Capture My Flag

Camp Clandestine
Book 1

K. L. Parsons

Also by K. L. Parsons

Stranded in Leavenworth Series

Love by a Landslide

Love Under Snowfall

Love on a Ledge

Camp Clandestine Series

Capture My Flag

Hearts and Crafts (coming soon)

 Formatted with Vellum

A Note From the Author About Trigger Warnings

Trigger Warnings: This book includes profanity, explicit sexual scenes that include the following; masturbation, oral sex, hair pulling, consensual voyeurism, light bondage, penetrative sex, and shaming. It is intended for mature audiences.

While it is my deepest desire to have the world read and love my stories, I am aware that some content may not be suitable for everyone. If any of the above is triggering for you, Capture My Flag may not be the right fit. Take care of your mental health—Leilani and Hudson still get their happy ending whether you make it through to the end or not. Enjoy!

Prologue

Four Years Ago: Leilani

"Look, if she doesn't like it, she's free to leave," the corporate douche drones, his voice grating my skin like nails on a chalkboard. The perfect wave of his dark brown hair flops over his forehead in that manufactured bedhead look these guys always seem to sport. You know the style: it's meant to look roguish and low-maintenance but ironically takes a solid hour to perfect. "Frankly, with what I'm pulling in these days, I can do better."

It didn't take much for my friend Bianca to sell me on spending a week at Evergreen Adventure Camp. I'd always wanted to attend summer camp as a kid, so the adult version was an instant yes for me. The perfect vacation and exactly what I needed to clear my mind and sort out some heavy relationship decisions.

Plus, the more I read through the brochure, the more

stoked I was to see they had archery, campfires, and a swim-mable lake. But what really snagged my attention—and what Bee intentionally marked with a sticky note because she knows me so well—was the capture the flag tournament. I'm in the middle of five athletic siblings, which means competition flows through my veins. Once I left home for college, I quickly learned the importance of reigning in those impulses to win at all costs so I didn't seem like "too much." To this day, I still tamp down the bloodthirsty urge in favor of a more team-oriented and harmoniously focused mindset, especially since I work as the program director at Tahoma Teen Center. It's on me to show the kids we serve all about winning and losing with grace and humility.

But here, at a summer camp specifically for adults? My guess is all bets are off, and I can let the real me out to play. Or better yet, let her out to conquer.

Plus, Bee keeps saying how awesome her camp friends from last year are, how I'll fit right in and love them too. I'm always down to make new connections.

Typically.

What my *lovely* friend didn't tell me—and swears she didn't know before arriving—was that her camp buddies were bringing a new person too.

So instead of allowing myself to sink into the care free fun, I'm stuck listening to this narcissistic asswipe as he brags about stock options and his recent "dope" promotion.

"Hey, man, you're being pretty harsh. This is Jessica you're talking about." Bianca's friend Charles (who is actually pretty cool so far) chastises in a way only a best friend can. "You've been together for nine years."

"Yeah, well," ass-hat scoffs, "maybe it's been eight and a half too long."

"*Hudson*," Charles scolds, recoiling like he's been jabbed in the chin.

Suddenly, an insistent ringing fills the air. The shrill sound ruins the ambiance of the campfire and the lilting, albeit off-key, rendition of "Two Princes" some dude is fumbling his way through on the acoustic guitar.

The smarmy worm pats his pockets until he locates the little flip phone contraband he slipped through at check-in. Because of course an entitled prick like him would ignore the camp's no electronics rule.

Charles starts to say something but cuts off as his friend holds up a finger and answers the call with a pretentious, "Go for Pratt."

This isn't how I expected the first night of summer camp to go. But as the shit stain who has a strikingly similar personality to my fiancé marches down a darkened path barking at some poor lady named Marjorie about the annual budget, I'm struck with something I haven't had in over a year.

Blinding clarity.

Chapter One

Four Years Later: Leilani

"Aren't we all a little too old for a panty raid?" My friend Melody drolls while wrestling with her rolling suitcase. The little wheels rebel against the pea gravel lining the path and lock up every few steps. Eventually, she gives up and leaves matching divots as she drags the luggage through the rocks.

Bianca halts so abruptly that Melody nearly trips over her feet. "Who are you calling old?"

"I'm not saying we're *old*, old," Melody says. "Only that the idea of grown men breaking into our cabin to steal our underwear seems a little on the nose."

"You mean like we're at a summer camp or something?" I tease over my shoulders, refusing to slow my pace. I've learned from past years that getting to the cabin after the other women sucks. Most of the bunks are great, but there's that one creaky relic that no one wants and I'll move heaven and earth to keep from being stuck with it for the second summer in a row.

My friends resume walking behind me, doubling the speed of their strides to keep up with my long legs.

"Sure, but it's more like a retreat." The edge of uncertainty in Melody's voice makes me smirk. "They call it a summer camp to be cute, right?"

Bianca, who manages to catch up with my breakneck pace, throws me a guilty look. "Maybe we should have filled her in beforehand?"

"She wouldn't have come otherwise," I whisper. "Mel needs this. She's done nothing but work, run, and binge old episodes of *Buffy the Vampire Slayer* since the divorce was finalized."

"There's nothing wrong with a routine, Leilani Walker," Melody hollers from a few strides back. I swear that woman's hearing is next level.

"Unless you're using it as a shield to hide behind," I counter.

"I'm taking my time. Easing into it."

"You didn't see Lance easing into it when he started dating his business partner." I'm aiming for tough love this time because the kid-glove approach hasn't been working. Melody married her college sweetheart shortly after graduation. They were happy for a long time, until Lance contracted a severe case of midlife crisis. One day, he came home with a shiny new crotch rocket, an appointment to get hair plugs, and divorce papers. "Dude barely waited for the ink to dry before he dove back into the dating pool."

The silence that follows makes me flinch.

I turn to see one of my best friends standing in the middle of the well-worn path staring down at her feet as she nudges a little pinecone with the toe of her hiking boot.

Shit.

The last thing I want is to hurt my friend's feelings by reopening old wounds—or, rather semi-fresh wounds. And while *I* would have already moved on if we'd swapped spots, clearly pushing Melody down that same route isn't the best plan.

Maybe I should put the kid gloves back on.

But only one.

"We'll meet you at the cabin," I say to Bianca, knowing she's antsy to get her things put away so she can connect with her yearly hook-up buddy. She doesn't even wait for me to finish my sentence before she sprints across the lawn and into cabin number six. She opens the door just as another gaggle of women approaches the front porch with luggage in tow. I wince, already knowing my springy fate for the next five nights, and leave my suitcase to backtrack toward Melody. "I'm sorry. That was harsh."

She shrugs. "Yeah."

There's zero resistance when I pull her in for a hug. Instead, she wraps her arms around my middle and clings to the back of my shirt. She sniffs once. Twice.

But before I can feel like the biggest jerk for making my

friend cry, she surprises me by asking, "Is that a new perfume?"

I chuckle, relieved that her sniffs were to smell me and that I didn't completely break my friend at the start of our first vacation together in nearly a decade. "New deodorant. Something with tangerine and vanilla."

She shimmies down and takes a bigger whiff of my armpit. "You're like a creamsicle."

"Count on you to make it awkward." Honestly, though, the whole exchange offers a fresh wave of sentimentality that soothes me from the inside. "I'm sorry for my comment. The last thing I want is to make you feel crappy after everything."

Melody pulls back and gives me an understanding smile. "I know you weren't trying to be mean. And you're right. I need to move on. Wallowing's a waste of time."

"Cheers to that. You ready to head in?"

She nods and grabs hold of her suitcase. I snag mine as we walk side by side toward our sleeping quarters for the next week.

The floorboards of the porch creak beneath our boots. By the sound—and look—of them, the planks are probably as old as Evergreen Adventure Camp itself. I scan the familiar semicircle of six weathered cabins arranged around a small fire pit and some Adirondack chairs. The spicy, crisp scent takes over my senses as the midday sun warms the cedar shingle siding.

This is my fifth summer attending the adult camp, and I'm still grateful that Bianca dragged me along the first time around. It took some convincing, and the visits haven't been without their flaws, but there's nothing like ditching your responsibilities and embracing some outdoor shenanigans. Hopefully, Melody sees it the same way and leans into the chaotic fun.

I push through the front door and am nearly knocked down by Bianca as she bolts past us and onto the patchy gravel path.

"See you at the opening ceremonies!" she shouts without turning back. We watch as she hurries toward the docks and dodges other campers who meander along the trail.

"Someone's an eager beaver," Melody comments.

I chuckle. "Now who's a little too on the nose?"

She rolls her blue eyes at me in mocked exaggeration but ends the gesture with a cheeky smile. This glimpse of my old friend—the happy version before her ex destroyed her confidence—warms my heart. No doubt this time away, breaking her from her princess-locked-away-in-a-high-tower routine, will do her some good.

"Let's get settled real quick and then I'll show you around. Activity sign-ups start in an hour," I say as we enter the cabin. The large main room that makes up most of the building is modest and exactly what you'd picture for summer camp lodging. Five sets of wooden bunks line the walls with a thin, plasticky, twin-sized mattress in each bed. No sheets and no pillows, which is why we were all told to bring our own.

On the far wall are two doors, one for the bathroom that houses a toilet, sink, and tiny shower. The other's a utility closet flush with brooms, dust pans, and other cleaning supplies we'll need to straighten up upon our departure. And between those two doors? A single, metal bed.

My bed, most likely.

Sure enough, Mel and I are the last to arrive. Every other wooden bunk has been claimed, aside from the top one nearest to the bathroom. Since my friend is already twitchy about the whole vacation as it is, there's no way I'm going to sequester her to the shitty, springy, back punisher.

"You take that one," I say, nodding to the last available wooden bunk.

"What if I want that one?" She points to the bed that a counselor sleeps on when the camp is used for children.

"Trust me," I sigh, tossing my suitcase on the mattress. The bed squawks in protest. "You don't."

Chapter Two

Hudson

An empty blue Nalgene dangles from my fingers as I walk onto the main field at the center of Evergreen Adventure Camp. It's surreal to be here again, like it's been both years and mere days since I last attended. Call me corny, but this has been the only place to bring me real, honest joy in the last handful of years. Back home, life's a grind. I typically spend too much time working—in the office and at home—and on the rare occasion that I take a day off, my mind won't focus on anything other than my latest project. It's cost me friendships and romantic relationships. Eventually, it started to affect my overall health. But it's how I'm wired.

Until I come here.

Because here, I log off. Completely.

At my first visit four years ago, I balked when they demanded my phone during check-in.

"I'm sorry, Mr. Pratt, but there's no tech allowed at camp," the lady at the registration table stated plainly, holding out her hand for my lifeline to the outside world.

"But what if someone calls?"

"I assume you have voicemail." Her sweet smile and the glint in her eyes hinted at the underlying pleasure she took from the exchange.

Charles had warned me about the electronics detox ahead of time. For a moment, I thought he was screwing with me, but ultimately I bought a cheap backup in case he wasn't. I cringe at how past-me handled my first stay at camp. If there had been a competition for the biggest douchebag here, I would have taken home the first, second, and third place ribbons, no contest.

It's been a gradual process, but I've changed over the years. Moreso, over the last six months, to be perfectly transparent. So, this time around, I'm all too excited to ditch my device. I'm determined to let camp heal me.

I *need* it to heal me.

A whole week of fun, relaxation, and not-so-friendly competition with my rival is bound to be just the ticket.

"Hudson!" a familiar baritone calls through the crowd.

I scan the field filled with booths where eager campers sign up for activities and spot my buddy Charles standing in line to fill his water bottle. He waves at me as I trot to his side.

"Hey, Chuck." I grin and bump my best friend's fist with my own. "Good to see you. How long have you been here?"

"Eddie and I got here about an hour ago. But dude was off in a blink the second his bag hit his bunk." Charles waggles his eyebrows. "Three guesses where he went in such a hurry, and the first two don't count."

I shake my head as the line for the water filling station moves up; I am in no way surprised that Eddie went looking for his "camp girlfriend" before doing anything else. "If that boy isn't careful, he's going to catch real feelings for her."

"*Going* to catch feelings? If you ask me, he's already a lost cause."

"Hey. No cuts!" a woman snarls from a few people behind us in line.

Neither Chuck nor I need to turn to know exactly who the holler came from.

Leilani Walker.

Speaking of lost causes.

My pulse quickly accelerates as I step out of line and approach the yearly bane of my camp existence. The thundercloud to my summertime fun. My arch nemesis for the week.

And my secret crush.

"Fancy seeing you here, Leilani." I try my best to ooze calm pleasantness, but I can't help the slight waver in my tone. "I would have thought you'd had enough after last year's embarrassment."

"The only embarrassment I see here is you, Hudson," Leilani says, crossing her arms tightly across her chest.

Of course I glance down at the extra cleavage she's created with her gesture. There's no helping it. I'm a moth to a flame. A flame I'd happily sink into if ever given the green light. Unfortunately, all this dazzling woman has ever flashed me is red, red, red. And honestly I'm not surprised.

"You can fling barbs all you want," I say as I step in a little closer and tower over her. She's tall for a woman, but I'm tall for a guy. She squints up at me, so I pluck the sunglasses off her head and plop them in place over her glare. "It doesn't change that last year, I won and you lost."

It's nearly impossible to remain still when she jabs me in the chest with her pokey fingernail, but I manage. Barely.

"Winning's easy when you cheat."

I'm not surprised by her accusation. It's the same song and dance she put on at last year's closing celebration. Still, I've worked hard to become an honorable man, and it gets under my skin when anyone accuses me of being anything but. The only comfort is that I'm certain I rankle her more than she does me.

Beside Leilani stands a little blonde wearing a ridiculously joyful grin. Her eyes oscillate between the two of us as we huck fightin' words back and forth. She's not familiar; I'm certain I'd remember all those curves if I'd met her last year.

"Who's your friend?" I ask, deciding to change the subject. I reach out to shake the new chick's hand until Leilani smacks it away.

"She's off-limits." A fiery pink washes over my rival's bronze cheeks, and it lights me up inside. Of all the activities

I've experienced at camp, picking on Leilani Walker like I just hit puberty is by far my favorite.

"Hudson!" Charles calls to me from the front of the line. "We're up."

"It's been a pleasure, ladies, but a man's gotta hydrate." I tap my empty Nalgene and join my buddy at the orange, plastic watercooler. He caps his bottle as I fill mine.

"Why do you feel the need to mess with that poor woman so much?"

"She asks for it, and what can I say? I'm a giver." Even as I joke, I'm simultaneously trying to quiet my thundering heart by mentally counting down from twenty.

Charles chuckles and claps a hand on my back. "Looks like she's in a giving spirit too. As in she wants to give you a black eye."

"Oh, no doubt." I'm under no delusion that Leilani wouldn't take the opportunity to destroy me if given half the chance. So my game plan is to *keep* her from getting the chance. Even if I like the idea of her whooping me a bit more than I let on.

Chapter Three

Leilani

"So that's the infamous Hudson, huh?" Melody asks.

I watch as he and Charles mosey away from the water cooler. If looks could kill, Hudson would have two eye darts protruding from the back of his neck. I tear my glare away and refocus on my friend. No matter how much Hudson Pratt pisses me off, or how badly I want to smack those dimples off his face, my mission this year has nothing to do with him. Mel is my mission. Her having fun and forgetting all about her shitty ex-husband for at least the next week is all that matters.

"Yep," I say. "That's him in the evil flesh."

"He's hotter than you made him out to be," Melody says casually, but of course I overreact.

My mouth drops open in shock, and I have to clear away

the harpy squawk before words have a chance to emerge. "Lusting over the enemy? Really?"

"Hey, this is my first time here. He's not *my* enemy." She teases while screwing the cap off her water bottle.

Finally, it's our turn at the cooler. I swipe the accumulating sweat from my brow as Mel fills her bottle. Wearing my hair loose was a bad idea. Twenty years ago, when I moved from Kona to Seattle for college, I wouldn't have batted an eyelash at letting it flow freely in the August heat. But after a couple decades living in a state with notoriously chilly, wet winters, I find myself less and less tolerant of hot, muggy days. When I head back to Hawaii to visit my folks I'm an even bigger wuss, a fact they both think is hilarious. I secure my heavy hair into a ponytail with the scrunchie on my wrist and flash a warning look to Mel.

"He's *my* enemy. You and Bianca are my best friends." I lean down and place my bottle beneath the spout. "Therefore, he's both of yours by proxy."

"Fine, fine," she acquiesces, hands in the air. "I'll play along with your silly vendetta."

I nod approvingly, glad to have that matter ironed out, and then immediately scowl as the stream of water comes to a stop.

"Nooo," I groan, pulling the top off the cooler. Some ice remains, but the water has run out. A low growl escapes my throat as I hurl another eye-dart at Hudson's back. I barely make him and Charles out in the crowd. "It's empty."

Melody goes up on tiptoes, looking around for someone to help. "Who do we ask to refill it?"

"We don't."

"Don't what?"

"Have someone do it for us. Camp rule: if you drain the cooler, you fill the cooler." I hand her my water bottle and snatch the big jug off the table. The line behind us groans impatiently as I waddle toward the kitchen. "Hold your horses, campers," I bark a bit too harshly; I should be directing my anger at the jerk who cut the line. If Hudson had followed the rules, my bottle would have been full and the chump standing behind Mel and me would be on refill duty.

***

"Have you decided what you want to sign up for?" I ask Melody after the cooler is filled and returned to the hydration station. We step farther onto the field, where a dozen tables are positioned in two rows. I have my preferred activities, but I plan to go along with whatever she's interested in checking out.

"I hadn't really given it much thought," she lies. Mel is a chronic over-preparer. There's no way she doesn't already have an hour-by-hour schedule mapped out for herself. "What do you and Bianca usually do?"

"Bee tends to sign up for whatever her boy toy does, and then they barely show up because they're too busy fucking each other's brains out. I'm a bit more dedicated to my selections: morning swim, archery, and—my favorite because I can cram Hudson into the dirt—CTF, capture the flag."

Melody balks as I ram the knuckles of one hand into the palm of the other.

"Oh," she says nervously. "Capture the flag doesn't really sound like my jam, but I guess I could give it a try."

"No, no, no. We're going to do what you want this year."

"Even if I pick arts and crafts or foraging?"

"Even if you pick arts and crafts or foraging," I assure her, wondering if she catches the twitch of my eye. Both of those sound awful, but if she wants to do them, I'll be with her the whole way.

My friend shakes her head and smiles. "That's sweet, but I don't need you to go along with whatever I want out of some erroneous sense of duty. I'm a forty-two-year-old divorcee, not some kidnap victim who spent fifteen years in a bomb shelter."

My snort laugh draws a few looks from nearby campers. "I see *Buffy* isn't the only show you've been binging."

"Hey, *Kimmy Schmidt* gets me, okay?" Melody loops her arm through mine and leads me up toward the end of the tables. "My point is, I don't have to cling to either of you to have a good time."

"You sure?" I ask, hoping she's being honest with me so I can skip foraging with a clean conscience.

"Definitely. Though the morning swim sounds like perfection; I'll do that with you. But that gives you the opportunity to still play capture the flag."

My heart begins to race.

I'd dismissed the idea of participating this year because I knew Melody would shy away from the competition. Now that I've been given the go-ahead, some fizzy emotion that I can't quite pin down fills my chest. Maybe it's elation or determination. There might even be a small sliver of nerves mixed in. But all I know is that the sensation grows as we saunter toward the booth to sign up.

"Hey, Leilani. It's good to see you again," greets the bubbly redhead running the capture the flag sign-ups.

"It's great to see you too. Bianca and I brought a new camper this year. Melody, this is Astrid. She's our favorite counselor," I explain, pulling my friend up to the table.

"Aww. I'm your favorite?" Astrid's grin widens, which doesn't seem possible. Then she leans in and whispers, "You and Bianca are my favorites too." She turns to Mel. "Pleased to meet you. Your friend's a camp legend."

Melody chuckles. "That wouldn't have anything to do with her competitive spirit, would it?"

Astrid nods, pushing a clipboard across the table to my antsy hands. "She's cutthroat."

My chest puffs up with pride. It's not that I need to be intimidating, or a winner, or the best . . . well actually, that's exactly what I strive for. Even though I haven't taken home all the CTF trophies over the years, I've still broken a couple of camp records. This time, I plan to do the same while also securing the win and making a certain smug asshole eat his words.

"I'm not surprised," Mel replies.

"Are you joining in too?"

"Oh no," my friend emphatically shakes her head and waves her arms in front of her. "This is so not my scene.

Besides running, I'm less the athletic and more the artsy type."

"Then you'll have to sign up for arts and crafts," the sunny counselor says and points across the way. "We have a new counselor teaching this year. He's not at sign-ups, but you'll meet him tomorrow at the first session."

"We'll head there next. Thanks, Astrid," Melody says with a winning smile.

I scribble my name on the next available space before scanning the list of other campers who've already signed up. Hudson's name glows like an obnoxious beacon at the top. Of course, he had to be the first to sign up. I glance at Melody and Astrid, who are still chatting, and take the opportunity to strike. The little penis I doodle next to his name is well-rendered if you ask me; complete with veins and squirrely hairs on the balls. It's sure to piss him off tomorrow.

Chapter Four

Hudson

I grumble aloud to myself, having drawn the short straw, and make my way down to the boathouse, where the canoes, paddleboards, and kayaks are stored. Activity sign-ups are done, and it's just about time to gather for the opening ceremonies. Charles and I got all the activities we wanted scheduled, but we haven't seen hide nor hair of Eddie. He doesn't care much for the activities since he rarely goes to them, but he'll be pissed if he misses the killer barbecue that happens after the camp owners and staff welcome everyone.

As I near the old wooden building, I listen for moans or rustling or any sounds that might indicate that my friend is balls deep in his camp fuck buddy. But all I hear is the gentle lapping of the water beneath the pier. Either they're between sessions or have found a new rendezvous spot.

The slatted door gives way with a creak as I push through into the main storage room.

"Eddie. You in here, man?" I call out quietly.

No response.

Aside from silence, there aren't any other signs that anyone's hooked up in here. No clothing flung anywhere, condom wrappers, or empty beer cans. I almost turn to leave.

Almost.

But then I hear movement in the room that holds spare life vests.

"Fuck me," I groan, rubbing a hand down my face. I call out again. "Hey. Eddie."

There's still some rustling, but nothing that indicates whoever is on the other side hears me.

The hinges of the rickety door I originally entered through creaks open, and I fling around to see a couple of campers hauling in a canoe. They're dripping water and laughing as they replace the watercraft on the appropriate rack.

"Hey," one of them says to me, inclining his head in greeting.

I respond with a two-finger salute from my forehead and an awkward grin. "Just um . . . deciding between a paddleboard and a kayak."

Canoe guy number two gives me an equally awkward thumbs up while also skeptically eyeing my hoodie and jeans. I'm not dressed for water sports, but I commit to the bit by reaching for a paddle and pretending to test its balance. Are paddles even supposed to be balanced? I haven't the foggiest idea, but I check for it anyway.

They must buy it because they drop off their gear and hastily leave the boathouse.

I sigh in relief and replace the plastic oar to resume my search for my friend.

"Psst. Edward," I hiss through the door and lightly rap on the wood with my knuckles.

Nothing.

"Fuck this." Completely over the caution, I barge into the room and stop dead.

Bent over a giant rolled-up string of buoys is Bianca. She jerks her head up to see who's walked in, eyes wide with shock. She has a knotted rope crammed between her teeth and tied around the back of her head. Each wrist is fastened with more rope to the circular metal frame that holds the string of buoys. At first glance, I don't see my friend. Bianca tries to shout some word that sounds like *Snuffleupagus* around the square knot filling her mouth. For an instant, I wonder if she's in distress, but then Eddie pops up from between her cheeks.

"What's wrong, baby?" he asks her, but trails off when he spots me. He doesn't bother hiding his erection. Instead, he wipes his forearm across his mouth, rests a hand on his hip and grins. "Oh, hey, Hudson. Good to see you, man. I'm a little busy, but we can catch up at dinner, okay?"

Like I said, I drew the short straw.

I turn, aiming to give them both a little privacy. "The

opening ceremony is about to start, so you've got about thirty minutes until the barbecue."

"Oh shit, that went by fast," he muses.

Bianca agrees with a muffled, "Uh-huh."

I'm back in the main room by this point and only pause because Eddie hollers, "Shut the door, will ya?"

CHARLES BARKS out a laugh that seems to go on and on. Tears stream down his face as he braces his hands on his knees.

"Sure," I scoff. "You think it's funny; meanwhile, I'm scarred for life."

"Oh, come on. Don't be such a prude," he chastises me through lingering giggles. "Just because you've been dry doesn't mean we have to be."

I ignore the sting of his comment. "I don't care what they do in private. Private being the operative word. A counselor could have walked in."

"So?"

"So, it would suck for him to get booted from camp," I insist, only they've been caught before, and no one seemed to care. And they're not the only ones hooking up around here. There's a reason everyone jokingly calls this place Camp Clandestine.

"He's a big boy—"

"I can attest to that," I interject quietly.

"My point is, maybe you should worry a bit more about

yourself and less about what Eddie is doing or where he's doing it."

Charles isn't wrong. While the last six months have been . . . transformative, I still have a lot more to work on. Worrying about how others spend their time isn't my business.

I shake the chip off my shoulder and ask my friend how things have been for him. As he starts to recount the latest drama of his weekly pick-up basketball game, the speakers spark to life with an ear-piercing squeal. The crowd of campers wails in complaint.

"Whoops, sorry everyone," Astrid, the managing counselor, chuckles. She taps the microphone a few times before continuing. "Welcome, everyone, to another summer at Evergreen Adventure Camp!"

This time, the crowd erupts in whoops and applause. A cluster of campers even begins chanting "Camp Clandestine, Camp Clandestine!" One of the guys in the group, with his arm flung around some chick's shoulders, steps behind her and begins thrusting in time to the chant. She must be his girlfriend or fuck buddy because she plays along, bending over and giggling into both her hands. Despite the overtly debaucherous pantomime, genuine excitement hums through me and I can't help but welcome the vibes as I soak it all in.

"I'm excited to introduce you to this year's staff members." Astrid flaps her hands to calm the crowd while struggling to contain her amusement. She then calls out names as each counselor steps forward to wave. Aside from a few newbies, I recognize everyone. "You may notice that two very important people aren't up here with us. Hank and Jolly Beaumont, the owners of Evergreen Adventure Camp, have finally retired. But worry not. The fun will continue with the Beaumont family. Hank and Jolly passed the camp down to their grandson, who plans to maintain the same lively and joyous atmosphere for years to come. So, put your hands together in a big camp welcome for Russell Beaumont."

A few campers clap half-heartedly as a giant dude trudges onto the stage. His massive hiking boots thud on the wooden planks of the mess hall's deck, a few of which seem to crack under the weight of him. His thick black beard, while trimmed with a shapely mustache, is long enough to graze the second button of his red and black buffalo plaid shirt. It appears he's tried to tame the thick black hair on his head with little success. I've never seen a lumberjack in real life, but this guy is a living, breathing caricature of one.

He stops beside Astrid, who projects a beaming smile at him. She gestures silently to the microphone, gently at first, but becomes more insistent as he refuses to approach it. Finally, she picks up the whole stand and places it in front of him. She mutters something to him, the edges of her grin faltering ever so slightly.

We all watch. No one makes a sound. Until finally the beast of a man opens his mouth.

"I'm Russell. If you need anything"—he rumbles and then throws a thumb in the managing counselor's direction —"talk to Astrid."

He turns and stomps back the way he came.

"That was something," Charles mutters to me with a low chuckle.

I nod, a little taken aback by the whole exchange. "Does he seem familiar to you?"

My friend mulls that over and offers a slight shrug. "The name does a little."

Astrid returns to the mic and claps her hands cheerfully. "Let's hear it for Russell."

A few people clap along with her, but the majority shuffle awkwardly and murmur to one another. Finally, the cheery redhead launches into a recap of all the new offerings at camp this year, including mermaid school at the dock—hard pass. Meanwhile, the enticing scent of smoky meat and fresh cornbread has my belly rumbling, and I casually wonder if I can have an extra helping if Eddie doesn't show up in time.

Chapter Five

Leilani

"Would someone please put that guitar out of its misery?" I bemoan to Bianca, who's making a rare appearance at campfire this evening. She claims her attendance is in honor of Melody's first night at camp, but I'm not buying it. Bee nods, only half listening to my complaint because she's too busy eye fucking Eddie, who sits across the flames between Hudson and Charles.

"I think he's pretty good," Melody provides between warbles of "Sweet Caroline." She sways next to me, holding a red plastic cup, letting the music and crackling logs do their mystical healing thing. I smile at her, willing to overlook the off-key singing and bad guitar playing if it means she's feeling light and happy for once. Regardless of how much it sounds like the musician is strumming with hot dogs instead of his fingers.

"Are you having fun today?" I ask Mel.

"So far, so good," she assures me. "But I have to say I'm a little skeptical of the cabins. That's a lot of grown women packed into one space."

I chuckle and nod in agreement. "It took me a minute to get used to my first year here. Sharing one bathroom with ten other chicks is the hardest part to manage. Especially in the mornings."

"Has there been bloodshed?" Mel asks a bit too gleefully.

I give her a judgy gaze. "No blood. Verbal assaults only."

"Wasn't there supposed to be a communal shower area?"

"There is, but it's way across camp, over by the guys' cabins," I lament. "Most of us make use of it at some point in our stay, but it's a long haul with soggy flip-flops and an overflowing shower caddy."

Bianca elbows me in the side, barely looking my way. "I'm gonna go grab a s'more kit."

"Oh sweet, will you snag me one?" I've been waiting to make my way to the table of ingredients that Astrid is manning. Hordes of people are crowded around her like scavengers, and I don't feel like charging my way through just yet. Plus, by the way the frazzled counselor keeps looking over her shoulder, I'm convinced whoever was supposed to help her didn't show.

"Me too, please," Melody requests.

"Sure, sure, be right back," Bianca mutters, still not looking at us. She rises from the log bench we're all sharing and saunters away from the campfire to the table of goodies. But instead of filling a plate with s'more fixings, she waits for

Astrid to turn to another camper and then swipes a jar of puffed marshmallow spread.

"Uh." I tap Mel on the arm. "I think we're on our own for s'mores."

"Why? What happened?"

I point to our friend, who tucks the container under her sweatshirt as she scurries down a path away from the campfire and into the darkness.

Mel giggles. "Someone's got a sweet tooth."

We watch as Eddie says something to his buddies, does a fake yawn, stretches, and heads down the same path.

"Sweet back of the throat's more like it," I joke, except I'm not joking. For sure, something's about to get smeared or dipped in that marshmallow spread. I physically shudder because all I can seem to focus on is how sticky it would be to have that shit somewhere on my body.

"I haven't even sat down and you're already cringing? That's brutal, Walker."

I whip around and see Hudson standing there with a paper plate in his hand. He lowers himself next to me on the log. Charles does the same, only he sits beside Melody. I'm not worried for her because, despite the shit company he keeps, Charles is a great guy. I've had the privilege of getting to know him over the last few summers.

"Do you *have* to sit by me, Pratt?" I ask scathingly, using his last name because, well, he started it. I turn. "Hey, Charles, how's the fam?"

He lights up with a grin so full of love. "Great. The twins started walking last week, and Aaron and I are exhausted from chasing after them. Honestly, I'm surprised he was cool with me coming this year."

"You have twins?" Mel asks happily.

"Two girls," Charles beams. He reaches for his back pocket then laughs in spite of himself. "I was about to show you photos, but no phone. You'd think after all these years of coming to this camp, I'd be used to it."

"I keep looking for mine too," she commiserates.

They continue jabbering away, and I turn back to my nemesis. Hudson smiles and holds his plate out to me. Two s'mores sit side by side in all their toasty-ooey-gooey glory.

"I brought you one."

"Why?" I snap.

He looks to the sky and thinks for a moment. "Call it a peace offering."

"I call it a trap."

"My, my, Leilani," Hudson tuts before setting the plate on his lap. He picks up one of the treats and breaks it in half. The marshmallow stretches as a glob of melted chocolate drops to the plate. "When did you become so cynical?"

"The day I met you."

"And how's that working out for you?" he asks.

I watch him take a big bite, giving zero fucks that the sloppy mess sticks to his lips. He licks it away after he swallows then raises his eyebrows and looks at me. "Have you decided your terms for this year's bet?"

"I have," I practically snarl. Hudson and I have been butting heads since the moment we met. I couldn't stand his douchey demeanor, and he couldn't stand me calling him on it. Our rivalry deepened quickly as we found ourselves on opposing capture the flag teams. Naturally, we made a wager about who would win. Spoiler: I did that first year. I'll never forget the grinding sound of his teeth as he watched me throw not one, but both of his cell phones into Heartbreak Lake. But this year, the stakes I've come up with when he loses are top-tier. "You're gonna hate it."

Hudson chuckles as he absently licks a sticky string of marshmallow from the corner of his mouth. "It's cute that you think you'll beat me."

"I have before," I press, staring longingly at the sloppy treat mocking me from his plate.

Fucking hell, I want that other s'more. What sucks is he knows it. But instead of smacking that smug smirk off his face, I accept the offering. I'm about to take a bite; the graham cracker is half an inch from my mouth when Hudson speaks up again.

"I made that one *especially* for you."

I halt and practically growl. "What's that supposed to mean?"

He only shrugs and then grins while his hazel eyes twinkle in the firelight.

Oh, how I loathe this man, let me count the goddamned ways.

With a frustrated grunt, I toss the s'more back onto his plate. He laughs. I fume. But I'm extra pissed as I watch him pick it up and shove half in his mouth.

"Like I would waste perfectly good, *un-tampered* with

food." Hudson pops the rest in his mouth then proceeds to suck the remnants from his thumb.

A tingling heat plays low in my belly, and I dismiss it as pure rage because it couldn't possibly be anything else.

Hudson chuckles, seemingly having gotten what he came for. He stands and faces his friend. "You ready to turn in?"

Charles shakes his head and laughs nervously as though he knows *exactly* who Hudson is messing with. "Right behind you. See you around, ladies."

Melody smiles and waves, mouth full of tasty s'more. At least she got one.

The guys leave the campfire area, as most of the other campers are doing. I head over to Astrid, holding out hope that she hasn't packed it in quite yet and that I can still get a last-minute treat. My heart sinks as I see a barren table aside from a few rogue grahams and empty marshmallow bags.

"Sorry," my favorite counselor soothes. Her once-neat ponytail is loose with frazzled strands of hair dancing around her face. A smear of chocolate stripes her neck from ear to clavicle. The woman looks wrecked but offers a giggle anyway. "They swarmed like locusts."

"Next time," I say, snatching bits of garbage to help her clean up.

"I thought the guys were bringing you and your friend some," Astrid muses while folding the sticky red checkered tablecloth.

"Like I'd trust anything from Hudson Pratt."

She laughs and checks her watch. "Barely the end of day one and the games have already begun, I see."

Four years ago, I knew the instant I met him exactly what kind of man Hudson was. Cocky, rude, and self-centered. Our first capture the flag face-off lit a fire in me, especially because my team won. Since then, our rivalry has intensified into something else entirely. The scent of flames and roasted marshmallows permeates the air, and I acknowledge exactly what's in store.

"It'll never be a game, Astrid. It's war."

Chapter Six

First Year of Camp: Leilani

I slip out of my sandals and step closer to the shore of Heartbreak Lake. The week was chock-full of adventurous campy fun, but Bee and I also made sure to include time for relaxation. Much of which took place here, lounging on a floaty as the gentle winds shifted us around the free swim area.

I've enjoyed so many aspects of camp, but the cozy body of water is about to top the charts as my all-time favorite place.

"Give 'em up, Hudson," I demand, holding out my hand.

"This is lame," the big baby grumbles. "I can't believe you're actually going through with it."

"Haven't you ever shaken on anything before?" My gaze sweeps over his irritated scowl and hunched, hoodie-clad shoulders as he steps beside me. He's full of regret, and he should be. "Even if I wanted to back out of the bet, *honor* requires me to follow through." I wiggle my fingers, which buzz with the anticipation of wrapping them around his precious tech.

"Oh, fuck off," he growls, slapping his little contraband flip phone into my palm.

"And the other," I coax as though I'm a preschool teacher trying to convince the class tyrant to give up the markers he swiped. I suppose it's not too far off from my interactions with a few of the kids at my teen center. But while they may be younger than Hudson, they sure act a hell of a lot more mature than this douchebag.

"No way." He crams his clenched fists into the pockets of his hoodie and takes a step back. "The deal was *a* phone. One."

His effort is commendable, but I'm an expert at side-stepping classic gaslighting tactics. "I assumed you'd say that. Charles?"

Hudson's best friend—and my favorite new ally—steps forward from the group of onlookers. He pulls a little spiral notebook from his back pocket and flips to a specific page. After clearing his throat, he reads the agreement aloud.

"If Hudson wins the capture the flag tournament, Leilani must dance the Macarena for the entire duration of the song during closing ceremonies in an outfit of Hudson's choosing. If Leilani wins the capture the flag tournament, she gets to dispose of Hudson's phones—see it says 'phones,' plural, right there—in any way she sees fit. And you both signed at the bottom." Charles tilts the pad first toward Hudson, then me.

"Thanks," I chirp, nudging my new buddy with my elbow. He grins at both of us, clearly tickled pink with the entire spectacle.

"It's been a privilege and"—he squeezes Hudson's shoulder—"my absolute pleasure to be of service."

"Screw you, Charles." Boy oh boy, someone's salty about settling his side of the bet. "Fine. Fucking take it. I'll just buy the newest model. Been meaning to upgrade anyway."

Hudson digs into his pants pocket and practically hucks his big-ass smartphone at me, then crosses his arms tightly over his chest and glowers.

"I guess it's a good thing you got that 'dope' new promotion." My cheeks hurt from smiling. I slip both of his phones into my back pockets and crouch to pick up a few rocks. In succession, I fling the pebbles as far into the lake as possible. I can feel the crowd behind us getting antsy; a few have already left.

"What are you doing?" Hudson bitches. The whine in his voice is morphine in my veins.

"Warming up." Another rock sails past the last two. "Don't wanna biff it."

"Leilani," Bianca calls, laughter tinting her words. "Quit playing with your food. Put the poor guy out of his misery already."

A few random campers murmur their agreement, and I

figured I've assaulted this douche canoe enough—time for the one-two punch.

"Any last words to your precious devices? We can record a video if you want."

Hudson stares blankly at me—sour-puss.

I shrug then grab hold of the flip phone first, haul back, and give a mighty heave. Warming up was the right call, because the old-school relic pops open in the momentum and flies end over end until it lands even farther than the rocks I threw.

"Nice throw," Charles calls. I know he and Hudson are friends, but I'm still not clear on the why of it all. Where Charles is kind, attentive, and laid back, his buddy is a rude, self-absorbed braggart. Bianca mentioned they'd known each other most of their lives, and I can't help but wonder if it's a friendship that's run its course.

"Thanks," I wiggle my hips in glee and turn to my newly acquired archnemesis. "Think I can get this one even farther?" I ask Hudson.

If smoke could come out of someone's ears, it would be pluming from his. He's so pissed off. Face red and pinched in distaste. He grinds his teeth together so aggressively that it sounds like the garbage disposal in my childhood home, which my dad had "fixed" five times before my mom finally convinced him to replace it. In other words, it sounds like gravel in a blender. Coming from him, it's the sweetest sound in the world, and I wish I could record it and use it as my ringtone.

"Will you please just do it already?" he growls.

"What is this?" I flutter a hand to my chest and gawk at Hudson. "I finally get a *please?*"

"*Leilani Walker*," Bianca snaps behind me. "Come on, girl, I wanna hit the road."

"Fine, fine," I lean over to Hudson, holding the phone out to him and whisper. "Perhaps you've suffered enough."

His hazel eyes light up as he looks from my face to his phone and back again. But as he reaches out to take it from me, I hastily hurl it through the air and into the murky abyss.

"Syke."

"You're the worst," he mumbles, then turns on his heels and marches toward the parking lot.

I watch him storm through the crowd of onlookers. A few campers leap out of his way to avoid being mowed down. Once I slip into my sandals again and leave the shore, Charles pulls me in for a hug.

"It was great meeting you, Leilani. Definitely the second-best part of this trip," he chuckles.

"Oh yeah?" I ask, accepting his friendly embrace and returning it in kind. "What was the best?"

"Watching you throw Hudson's shit into the lake. I can't wait to tell Aaron about it. He's gonna lose it." He grins so hard that there's a rosy flush on his deep brown cheeks. "But I'd better go. Hudson's my ride, and I'm not naive enough to think he won't leave my ass behind."

He hugs Bianca too then jogs to catch up with his friend, who's already snatched up his duffel bag.

Bee shifts closer and loops an arm around my waist.

"Wanna come back to camp next year?" she asks.

"Yep," I respond without hesitation. "I had a great time. Plus, bonus. . .There's no way Hudson-I'm-a-huge-asshole-Pratt will ever come back."

"You don't think so?"

"Nah. He doesn't strike me as someone who gets over humiliation so easily."

Chapter Seven

Present Day, Tuesday Morning: Leilani

The noise level in cabin six grows as the rest of the women in the building cheerily begin their day. Some get in line for the bathroom, while others climb into each other's bunks to chatter about the plans for the week. Breakfast isn't for another two hours, yet the excitement and energy have already reached a crescendo.

But not for me.

Nope. I'm lying flat on my back staring up at the ceiling. The only position I can maintain on this torture device and still hope for a few winks. At home, I'm a side sleeper, but here, any other position than the one I'm currently cemented into will result in the puncturing of a vital organ or two. Whoever clears this death trap for duty each year is either sadistic or negligent. I haven't decided which is more likely, despite the ample time to ponder this while lying awake for hours wishing for a sedative.

With all the strength—mental and physical—I can muster, I heave myself to roll off the edge of the bed and land on the wooden planks of the floor. The short tumble is jarring at first, but the lack of jabby metal springs means I can finally relax my body.

As I snatch my pillow from the cot and plant it beneath my head, a sweet chuckle flows in on a refreshing summer morning breeze.

"Comfy?" Melody asks, kneeling beside me. Her cheeks are flushed and sweat glistens at her temples.

"Now I am," I mumble, curling my knees to my chest and snuggling deeper into my pillow. I peek through one cracked eyelid and take in Mel's worried gaze. Her train of thought is blatant, but I'll have none of it. "No."

"I think we should swap," she declares anyway. "You know me, as long as I get my morning run in, I sleep like the dead."

"Besides last night, when was the last time you slept anywhere other than your bed at home?"

She gives it a hard consideration, and I almost laugh at how her face scrunches while she thinks. But laughing would no doubt revitalize the low back spasm I had from eleven fifty p.m. until one forty-five a.m. (yes, I checked my watch).

"I don't mind trading," she insists, getting to her feet and reaching down to help me to mine.

"But I do. This one's mine and that's the end of it."

"Fine, fine." Mel chuckles, holding up her hands and

backing away. "I'll drop it, but I'm happy to snuggle if you decide to crawl in with me one of these nights."

I smile warmly at my friend, strongly considering her offer to share as I brush the dirt off my pillow and return it to my shitty bed.

"An anonymous donor?" Mel asks as she serves herself a modest scoop of oatmeal and then drowns it with all the toppings. There's more brown sugar, cinnamon, dried fruit, and seeds than actual oats. The concoction looks pretty good, and I make a mental note to give it a try later this week. For now, I stick with my usual eggs, hashbrowns, and coffee.

"Completely anonymous. Five hundred dollars every month since the start of the year."

"I love it," she says with a grin. "Do you get a lot of donations like that at the teen center?"

"One-offs all the time." I snatch a mug from the rack and fill it with hot, bitter coffee. A few drops splash out and scald my fingers. I hiss, more from being startled than hurt, and wipe my hand on my jean shorts. "But typically, if they're recurring and substantial like that, the donor wants the credit for tax write-offs or clout. Also, our fundraisers add them to a database and send thank you cards, event invites, or whatever else to foster that relationship."

"So, it's an actual good deed," Mel muses with a beaming smile.

I follow her away from the buffet line and shrug. "I'd say so. Or as close as someone's going to get to one."

In the five years I've worked for Tahoma Teen Center, I've been blown away by the generosity of the community. The locals have shown up in a big way. We have a strong partnership with the school district and a number of influential local companies. Plus, it doesn't hurt that the mayor is so fond of programs like ours. She's always talking about the importance of strong, nurturing foundations for our youth in her speeches. But this type of donation, recurring with no name attached, is not the norm.

Still, I know what they say about gift horses, so I'll happily look the other way if it means the funds will continue to roll in.

"Good morning, ladies," Charles says from one of the long cafeteria tables. He grins from ear to ear. "Care to join us?"

Unfortunately, Hudson is sitting beside him. There's no way I can handle spending my first morning looking at his stupid face. Not after the night I had flopping around on my very own medieval torture table. But before I can explain that sitting too close to my nemesis before having my coffee will give me heartburn, Melody happily accepts and plops directly across from Charles. The two of them launch into a conversation about their spawn while I scan the room for open tables.

"Might hurt her feelings."

I glower down at Hudson, who's halfway through a bowl of oatmeal. I'd never openly admit it, but he's right. It's super important to me that this week goes well for Melody. She's been through some shit lately and deserves a drama-free week; she especially doesn't need drama to come from me.

Which is why I sit.

"Rest of the seats are full anyway," I grumble.

Hudson scans the mess hall, and I know full well he clocks an empty space or two, but he must have gained a few extra brain cells recently because he keeps his mouth shut and returns to his breakfast.

I take a long gulp of hot coffee to ward off my sleepiness then prepare to dig into my rehydrated scrambled eggs and hash brown patties, but feeling someone's eyes on me draws my focus.

"What?" I demand, fork an inch from my mouth.

"Nothing," Hudson assures me, obnoxious smirk tugging at his lips. He dips his gaze and scoops up the last of his oatmeal. He chews slowly, and I return to my bite until he speaks up again. "It's just. . ."

The eggs tumble off my fork and slap onto the sloppy heap I'd scooped onto my plate in the buffet line. My blood sugar is low, patience nonexistent, and this walking red flag is begging for a slow death.

"What?" I demand again, this time with twice as much venom.

"Did you sleep all right?"

If I didn't know any better, I'd think there was an edge of concern to his question. But having been well-acquainted with this bastard, I wait for the punch line.

"I slept fine," I assure him through a gritted smile. "Why do you ask?"

He shrugs, tossing his napkin and spoon into his bowl, and pushes to a stand.

Thank fuck. I can finally eat in peace. I hastily shovel a couple of bites as he says his farewell to Charles and Mel. As a bit of food settles in my belly, I can feel color returning to my cheeks, energy to my limbs. Soon I'll be enjoying the rest of my breakfast in peace, followed by a serene float on Heartbreak Lake for morning swim.

But instead of leaving, Hudson stops beside me. Even before he leans down so his mouth is close to my ear, I can smell the soap he used in the shower. I'd say Irish Spring, but there's a hint of woodsmoke like he's been standing near a campfire. "You look tired. Hope it doesn't throw off your game."

I miss the chance to tell him to eat a dick because I'm too busy taking in his lingering scent while he strides away to drop off his dishes.

Chapter Eight

Hudson

"Do we really need to wait for her?" I grumble at the new counselor wearing a wide-brimmed hat and an obscene amount of sunscreen. Streaks of zinc-infused paste slash across his face, making him appear even whiter than his orange hair would suggest. He fans himself with a clipboard and I notice droplets of sweat forming on his brow. In a matter of minutes those drips will slide through the kid's melty SPF coating and land right in his eyes.

Today is hot. And I mean *hot* hot. It's about three in the afternoon, and my balls are sticking to my legs. And we're all about to get even sweatier once we start running drills. That is, if a certain brat decides to grace us with her presence.

I pull the clipboard from our supervising counselor's hands and scan the names. Most I remember, but there are a few that are unfamiliar. Then my eyes land on the top of the page where I signed up. My lips pull into a scowl, knowing exactly who scribbled a cock and hairy ball sack next to my name.

"We still have five minutes," the gangly employee says with a huff while snatching the clipboard back from me. This kid can't be more than twenty-three or so. I would have guessed younger, but I've seen him around in years past. Plus, bar rules apply due to the fair amount of alcohol consumption that happens on the property. Even now, a few guys foolishly pass a flask back and forth.

Fucking newbies.

In this direct sun and heat exposure, I wager one or both will be puking within the hour. I make a mental note to ensure the wannabe frat bros end up on Leilani's team. The thought of her flipping out on her teammates while they succumb to alcohol poisoning fills me with a giddy pleasure. I can practically hear the venom in her voice and see the clench of her jaw and fists and ass cheeks as she trembles with outrage as bro-one and bro-two spew their guts out.

Warmth seeps through my chest. I press my sleeves up to my elbows and throw back a gulp of water to cool down.

Finally, the woman in question turns the corner of the path from the girls' cabins and trots to the field. Her long, dark braids bounce on her chest with each stride.

"Cutting it a little close, are we?" I scold, not really upset but wanting to mess with her as much as humanly possible.

She checks her watch, stops beside me, and tilts her wrist so I can see. "Look at that. It's fuck-you-o'clock. Appears I'm right on time."

A few campers who have witnessed our rivalry before snicker. One shouts that I've *been burned* then high-fives his buddy. Clearly, the bulk of the group is here for the spectacle of our feud just as much as the actual games.

"Real cute, Walker," I chastise playfully.

"Thanks." She gives me a mischievous smile and another wave of warmth engulfs my core. The scrunch of her freckled nose and tilt of her pink lips do something to me. I defy an impulse to trace the smattered constellation of flecks on her cheeks and resign myself to gently tug on the end of one of her braided pigtails instead. She slaps my hand away and takes a step to her left.

Apparently, camp reduces me to an overgrown preteen.

Back home—in my real life—if I found a woman attractive, I wouldn't hesitate to make a move. An *age-appropriate* move like asking her out for a drink. But here, I resort to pretending like I'm not into the hottest woman on site. Maybe I should take a page out of Eddie's playbook and suggest a standing fling with Leilani. Except I have no doubt she'd laugh at me and use the proposition to mock me until I leave and never return. Something about maintaining this combative rivalry lights my fire—motivates me—and the last thing I want is for it to end.

Especially amidst the uncertainty back home.

"Is everyone ready to get started?" Sergeant Sunblock asks the group. He's wiped his eyes with the back of his arm and is now squinting from the sting of salt and lotion.

The group hoots and hollers, including Leilani. She hops from foot to foot and throws her hands into the air. So naturally, I drink my fill of her bouncy tits and exposed abdomen while she cheers in excitement.

"I'm Clark." The young counselor presents his badge like he's a fucking FBI agent. "I'll be overseeing the capture the flag events. We're going to form two teams. Do we have volunteers for captains?"

Leilani's hand shoots into the air, gifting me another glimpse of her soft, tan middle. In the afternoon sunlight, I think I spy something sparkling on her belly button. Fuck. If she got it pierced, I might lose it. I swallow a groan and look to the sky.

"Hey, Pratt," her cheeky purr pulls my attention back to the activity. "You too chicken shit to lead a team this year?"

Her eyes glitter like she caught me mid-ogle.

Busted.

I cram my hands into the pockets of my hoodie and plaster a smirk on my face. "I thought maybe I'd give you a fighting chance and let someone else be captain, but—"

"Like I said," she interrupts. "Chicken. Shit."

I run my tongue along my teeth, making a big show of "deciding" whether I'm going to take the role or not, when we both know full well that I wouldn't pass it up. This is, after all, the exact reason I come to camp each year. It's the one week out of fifty-two that I truly enjoy—six glorious days where I come alive and vibrate from the sheer joy of being around this woman. We'd never work in the real world. No doubt we'd destroy each other (and not in the fun way). Shit, we probably wouldn't even work here.

But I'll take whatever attention I can get from Leilani Walker.

Even if all I get is scorn, sarcasm, and irritation.

"I suppose I could wipe the floor with you again this year." I shrug noncommittally, like I could take it or leave it.

"Right," Clark arches a brow and looks between us. Poor kid has no idea what he signed up to oversee. "So, Leilani and Hudson are team captains. How do you want to split up the—"

"I call Kendrick," Leilani shouts, jabbing a finger at the biggest, strongest person in the group.

Dammit. Kendrick was on my team last year and the guy was clutch for the win. Especially when it came to the obstacle event. Dude basically stood at the ready and threw teammates over the climbing all whenever they got stuck.

Whatever. I'm unbothered.

"Jemma," I call out. A sinister grin blooms on the tiny blonde's lips. Her teeth appear sharper than humanly possible, but that's probably because she's notoriously the type to go for the kill. What she lacks in size, Jemma makes up for in ruthless speed and sheer power. But I suppose teaching Krav Magga for well over a decade would turn anyone into a certifiable badass.

"Linda," Leilani says, continuing her team selection.

"Malik."

"Albert."

"Christina."

"Guy over there," Leilani points to one of the two bros who have been taking pulls from their flask.

"I'm Brad, but you can only have me if you take my buddy Chad too," the guy says, slamming a hand down on his friend's shoulder in solidarity.

Leilani looks over at me to see if I'm cool with that. The last thing I want on my team is two asshats chugging their cinnamon whiskey and nut tapping each other when they should be strategizing, but I don't want her to know that. So I school my features, *think it over*, and finally nod.

"As long as I get the twins," I demand. Last year, there was a little collusion between the identical brothers. They were split between the teams and had a hard time with the separation, so they decided to work together anyway. Fortunately, their loyalty was with my team. Unfortunately, Leilani bitched incessantly that the only reason she lost was because the twins and I cheated.

"Like I'd trust either of them on my team anyway." She crossed her arms and rolled her eyes aggressively. "Take 'em."

We divvy up the remaining campers and cluster in our respective groups to come up with team names.

"All right. Who should we be?" I ask, rubbing my hands together like I'm a super excited raccoon.

"The Tidal Waves," one camper offers.

"Team Big Foot," another chimes in.

I nod, enjoying the enthusiasm, but not sold on the suggestions so far. "Good start, what are some other options?"

"Saber-tooth Tigers?" the twins say in unison.

At this point everyone is chattering over each other, calling out every type of name under the sun.

"The Face Fuckers," Jemma offers, a little too calmly.

The group quiets, and all eyes turn to her in varying states of alarm. Someone chuckles behind their hand, and a few others take a step back.

"Solid name, solid name," I say carefully, placating to this woman who frankly scares the shit out of me. "But that might be a bit too aggressive. I doubt Counselor Clark would allow it. Why don't we vote?"

The palpable unease of the group is tough to shake, but when we finally decide on a team name, everyone seems to settle.

Clark calls us back together and gives a rundown of the rules. It's the same as every year. There are three events over three days. The first is a standard capture the flag game ending when one team returns to their home base with the other team's flag. The second is an obstacle course relay where each teammate must make it through a set of obstacles, collect one of the opposing team's flags, and return to the starting line. Finally, my favorite, because it's played at night, the multi-flag capture. Before the game starts, the counselors hide various flags all over the surrounding woods. Whoever collects the most in the allotted time wins.

"Does anyone have any questions?" We all look around and, surprisingly, no one raises a hand. "Cool. Then today, feel free to split off and run drills or do whatever you want to prepare. The studio in the Art Barn will be open after dinner until nine if you'd like to make a team banner, or paint matching shirts, or whatever. The first game starts tomorrow at three."

Leilani's teammate Kendrick stands beside her, dwarfing the woman with his sheer size as he leans over and whispers something in her ear. She claps a hand over her mouth to stifle a chuckle. Last year, Kendrick told me he owns a bar in Leavenworth, Washington, and now my self-flagellating mind is picturing him bending her over a keg in the walk-in. Jealousy swarms my chest like a mass of angry hornets.

"You wanna share what's so funny with the rest of the class?" I sneer. While I have no claim to her, I'm desperate to break up their little chitchat.

The group turns to me, clearly trying to suss out what my problem is.

Leilani speaks up. "Kendrick was asking if we'd already made our bet."

Now that her focus is back on me, my ire melts away, because that's all that I want.

To capture her attention. Be in her thoughts. Stay firmly at the top of her mind.

"Now's as good a time as any." I aim for smooth nonchalance as she swaggers over to stand right in front of me. "Ladies first."

She grins, showing teeth. "When I win, you can't wear hoodies for an entire year."

Diabolical woman.

If you ask my parents, they'll attest that I've never had a security blanket or a favorite stuffed animal. I didn't ever need one. But once I left for college, hoodies quickly became my comfort item. I wear them year-round and everywhere—

on dates, at the gym. I even keep one at the office so I can swap out of my suit jackets between meetings.

Or I used to when I had an office to go into each day.

Life has changed a lot in the last six months. *I've* changed a lot, but one thing remains the same—my hoodies.

But I won't let her know how hard the loss would hit me. Besides, I won't have to give them up because there's no way I'm losing.

I muster all the calm I can into a noncommittal shrug. "Fine."

She's almost fooled, but if I know Leilani—and I'd like to think I've gotten a pretty accurate pulse on her—she sees right through my casual air.

"Fine," she parrots, then smirks. "And *if* you win?"

"When we win, you have to propose to me at the closing ceremonies on Saturday morning."

"What?" she squawks. The others gasp and titter to each other.

"On stage," I pause for effect. "And on live stream so the world can see."

I love the shade of pink that washes over Leilani's face as she grits her teeth and clenches her fists so tightly, I expect her nails to draw blood. She's no doubt picturing herself knelt at my feet, a scenario I've fantasized about hundreds of times only in my case it's not to propose. Instead I imagine her licking her lips and clawing at my belt buckle. Now, I'm the one blushing just thinking about it and take another swig of water to hide my flaming cheeks.

After a moment, her shock wears off and she relaxes. And just like that, she's dismissed the notion that I'll beat her.

"Sure thing, Pratt." Leilani turns to Counselor Clark. "Do you want to hear our names?"

"Oh, right," Clark says, checking his watch like he's been over this whole thing for a while now. The counselor clears his throat. "Whatcha got?"

Instead of sharing theirs, Leilani gestures for our team to go first. I'm suspicious of why, but figure it doesn't really matter.

"We decided on the Tidal Waves."

"Cute," Leilani says. "Very intimidating."

It's my turn to roll my eyes. Personally, I don't love the name, but it was either put it to a vote or become The Face Fuckers. Going the democratic route seemed to be the safest bet. "What's yours?"

She grins like whatever they picked will irritate the hell out of me.

And she's right.

"We went with *Hudson Sucks*."

Chapter Nine

Leilani

"Paint the letters as big as you can," I urge. "We want to make sure everyone can see *Hudson Sucks* no matter where they're standing."

After Clark, the baby counselor, released our teams, we spent a couple hours talking about the game plan and running drills. Instead of anything strategically concrete, we're opting for more adaptable guerrilla warfare tactics. For the first event, anyway, it seems smarter to split up and come at the enemy from all sides.

I'm not surprised that we've already lost a couple players. Brad and Chad dipped when one of them started dry heaving during the fifth set of burpees. Crybabies. We're better off without them. Honestly, I'm relieved because the more dead weight we can trim before the obstacle relay, the better position we'll be in.

"Shit," I grumble when the nearly empty bottle of teal paint refuses to release its contents. A few shakes produce the final dregs, which also manage to splatter on my denim cutoffs. I try to wipe it off with my fingers, but they are just as coated, and I end up spreading it around instead of removing it.

"A few more colors and the smears on your shorts will start to look intentional," Melody says thoughtfully. Being the angel that she is, my friend offered to help with our team signs even though she isn't part of the event. During dinner, when I mentioned that I'd be in the Art Barn, she nearly choked on a tortilla chip. My best guess is that she has the hots for the art director, Everett, but getting anything out of her is like prying open a steel trap.

"Splatter paint jorts." I mull over the idea, intrigued that instead of considering them ruined, I could lean into the destruction and call it stylish. "I love it."

"Perfect. That means you can't be mad at me." Her words don't register right away because she says them so sweetly. But then my mind perks up.

"Mad about what?" I ask right as she slaps my ass with a squelchy whack. My yelp is partly from the sting she leaves behind, but mostly shock that she actually put an orange handprint on my back pocket. A quick twist and glance over my shoulder to inspect her handiwork has her giggling.

"I've got good aim, don't you think?"

She's right, and I can't be mad at her, not even a little because my friend who's been limping through life like a shell of her normal self is grinning with pure joy. Bringing her to camp was the right call. I mentally pat myself on the back.

"Am I going to have to separate you two?" The deep, flirtatious tone causes Melody's gleeful laugh to morph into an awkwardly hysterical chuckle. Everett deposits an armload of paint at the end of our table.

Whoa nelly, this man is a piece. He's about five years too young for me, but I can still admire the hell out of the genetics that combined to create him.

"We're cool here," I assure the art director. "She's just helping me turn my ruined shorts into a work of art."

"Very creative," the young Adonis praises Melody.

"It's whatever," she responds, clearly flustered. Her face is beet red. She absently tucks her blonde hair behind her ear with her painted hand and leaves a streak of orange at her temple.

"You've got a little. . ." Everett trails off and steps forward to cast the color away with a gentle swipe of his thumb.

I'm giddy watching the exchange, while also feeling like I've walked into something not for my eyes. There's a gentle intimacy in his action, and I'm riddled with more questions than my brain can organize.

"Thank you." Mel manages to flame even brighter under his touch.

"Anything for you," Everett insists, then turns to me. "Let me know if you need more supplies. I can raid the closet again."

Before I can close my mouth that's hanging open in awe, Mel spins on me. "Hush, you."

Is there something going on between you two? Why did he gently swipe away that paint? Have you kissed? Hooked up? Has there been naked time of any sort since we got here yesterday?

A bazillion questions bubble up my throat, but I swallow them down instead of word-vomiting all over my newly divorced friend.

"I didn't say a word." Despite wanting to. . .desperately.

"Your face says it all," she says, and then returns to the eight-foot-long *Hudson Sucks* banner I plan on bribing other campers with airplane bottles of booze to hold up during the events.

"Fine," I finally settle on, planning to sic Bianca on her later. If we see Bee again before the end of the week that is. Neither of us has spotted her or Eddie since the campfire last night. You'd think I'd be worried, but it's business as usual for them. Their camp rendezvous tends to emulate a week-long bender of screwing all over the property until Bianca shows up at the car on Saturday morning with twigs in her hair and scraped knees. I've checked around with some other campers and there have been sightings, so I'm confident she's happy as a clam.

"Make room."

My attention pops up from painting as Hudson walks over with a fistful of paintbrushes and his tidal wave of losers. Individually, I have nothing against any of the campers on his team, but since they're loyal to my nemesis, I gotta be a little snarky.

"Wait your turn, Satan," I say.

Hudson sets down his brushes and settles his hands on his hips, standing there rigidly with visible indignation. But there's also a slight smirk tucked on one side of his mouth. I zero in on it and flirt with the idea that perhaps he gets off on our antagonistic exchanges.

"Resorting to name-calling," he says and tsks. "Such childish antics are beneath you, Walker. Wait. Never mind. I forgot who I was talking to for a moment."

"Woopsie," I slap my hand over my mouth in mock mortification. "Did I give away your secret underworld identity? Everyone, hide your virgins. Oh wait. Hudson's probably the only one here."

"Move over," he says with exasperation.

"We got here first, Pratt. Use the floor or wait your turn." Ignoring him, I resume painting and turn to Mel. "Should we make the letters bigger? I want to be sure everyone can see *Hudson Sucks*."

"Leilani." My friend says my name in that long, drawn-out way parents use when their child is being a terror. Except in this case, I'm not Mel's sixteen-year-old son, who actually happens to be the best kid on Earth.

"What?" I double down, knowing full well I'm in the wrong. "If making his little sign is that important to him, he would have gotten here right after dinner like the rest of us."

I lean forward and flick one, two, three of Hudson's paintbrushes off the table. The sound of them clattering to the ground echoes through the silent room. Everyone is watching with rapt attention—I can feel the intensity of their stares—as they wonder what will happen next.

But my eyes are on my rival.

I fixate on the way he calmly removes his large hands from the pockets of the hoodie he'll lose by the end of the week and braces them against the edge of the sturdy table. Hudson leans forward. His eyes are dark with an almost sinister glint, like he's reached the end of his patience. About ready to snap.

He licks his lips and bares his teeth.

"Pick that up," he demands, low and so quietly I wonder if I've imagined it.

The shudder that runs up my spine is nothing short of titillating. Perhaps he's not the only one enjoying our feuding a little too much. But of course I refuse to yield. So instead, I lean forward, so close I can smell the lingering mint of his toothpaste, and raise my hand to shove another paintbrush off the edge.

"Make me."

Chapter Ten

Hudson

If I had been alone in the Art Barn with Leilani when this played out, I would have been around that table before the bouncing paintbrush settled on the ground. Standing toe to toe with her, so close she'd have to crane her neck to meet my eyes. She would too. There's no reality in existence where this woman would cower or back down or avert her gaze. But then I'd spin her around, bend her over the paint-smeared table. Her mocking laughter would echo in my ears as she took joy from having riled me up. Those little fucking shorts would ride up, and whispers of her cheeks would pop out the bottom. Begging to be spanked.

I'd give her one final chance to right the wrong and pick up the paintbrushes she flicked to the floor or else. But she'd be too obstinate for something like that. Instead she'd tell me to fuck off or call me chicken shit again, so of course I'd let her have it.

My hands pulse at the thought of landing my palm on her frayed back pocket.

"Earth to Pratt."

Leilani's mocking tone tunnels through my little disciplinary fantasy. A twinge of pain radiates from my fingertips. I have to command myself to release the death grip I have on the edge of the butcher block tabletop. I take a deep breath to settle my erratic heart and will the blood that's rushing to my dick to reverse course.

And naturally, that's when she reaches over to shove the final paintbrush off the edge of the table.

But I'm faster than she is.

My fingers curl around her wrist with lightning speed and hold her steadfast.

The gasp that parts her lips morphs into a breathy chuckle. Her pulse thrums wildly beneath my fingers. She looks at me through lowered lashes like she's almost glad I'm standing up to her. Like she's been pushing my buttons intentionally because she wants me to react to her.

To *physically* stop her.

She doesn't try to pull back. Instead, she shifts her wrist around like she's testing the solidity of my hold. Aiming to see what I'm capable of.

The room has gone eerily quiet. It's not until a masculine throat clearing breaks the silence that our stare down falters. The art director stands at the end of the table beside Leilani's friend Melody.

"I've heard tales of the legendary rivalry the two of you have, but let's keep it out of the Art Barn, shall we? We're all adults and even though it's summer camp and we're here to have fun, it doesn't mean we should act like children."

The art director's chiding request has a sharp cooling effect on the fire that's been licking at my insides, especially as he walks around the table and gathers the fallen paintbrushes. My jaw unclenches and I finally release Leilani's arm.

But I'm almost certain that I spy the dim of disappointment in her eyes just before she turns away.

"Sorry, Everett," she says with a forced calm that I can one hundred percent relate to.

"Yeah, sorry," I murmur, shoving my hands back into the pockets of my hoodie.

"There's plenty of room for everyone here. Hudson, let me clear off the back counter and you guys can work on your signs there," Everett offers, but Leilani cuts in.

"We're done here anyways." She looks to her friend. "Can you help me move the sign to the back room to dry?"

"Sure," Melody says hesitantly, grabbing one end of the clearly unfinished banner.

They carry it out of the main room and the rest of my team cautiously approaches the long worktable. By the time Leilani and Mel gather the rest of their stuff and walk out of the barn without a backward glance, we've all spread out and gotten to work.

Shit. Now I feel like an asshole.

Despite how it might have looked, I wasn't trying to get

either of them to leave. All I was doing was messing with her like usual. The studio is more than big enough for all of us to work on our signs and still maintain a bit of distance.

But now she's left.

Bottles of teal and orange paint line the end of the table where they'd been working. Her banner is unfinished, and the games start tomorrow.

I like irritating Leilani Walker. Love it, actually. But I don't feel right about her scurrying out with her tail between her legs.

A deep breath fills my chest as I try valiantly to expel the guilt. But alas it builds and will probably linger unless I do something about it. I have years of bullshit to atone for, and I'd prefer to keep from piling on. So, like the better man I'm trying desperately to become back home, I walk toward the back room. But not before scooping up the abandoned cups of paint and a few extra brushes.

Chapter Eleven

Wednesday: Leilani

"I'd stay and watch if I could, but I promised Everett that I'd help him with the art room disaster," Melody explains as she swipes teal and orange markings onto my cheeks.

"Trying to get a little one-on-one tutoring with the hot teacher, huh?"

Her lips purse in that motherly scowl Bianca and I have become accustomed to. Not because she ever has to direct it at her son. Alex is an angel. Really, the best teenager to ever exist. No, she saves her I'm-so-disappointed-in-you face for her two best friends.

And every single time it makes us giggle.

"It's not like that," she states plainly, but I can see the effort it takes her to keep her grin at bay. "We trashed the studio tie-dying shirts earlier, and we promised to help with the aftermath. A group of us will be there."

"But you wish it were just the two of you."

She doesn't respond, but I have my answer when she jabs my face a little too hard with a makeup sponge. The drag of the face paint tickles the side of my nose and I reach up to scratch before my friend can smack my hand away again. "Stop. You'll smudge my masterpiece."

"A couple of days in the Art Barn and already you're Picasso or whatever."

"Hey, it takes a real artist to work with any old medium."

"Are you referring to the paints or my face?" I ask, only feigning offense. "Because watch who you're calling old, ma'am."

Mel clicks her tongue and rolls her eyes in disapproval. "There's barely a laugh line to speak of, my dear."

"It's those collagen face masks you and Bianca got me for my last birthday," I say, trying to hold still while under the application. "It's torture sitting still while they soak in, but once I peel it off. Yowza."

"I told you," she tuts.

Self-care has never taken the front seat for me. Aside from daily vitamins and slathering on the sunscreen, I keep my routine to a minimum. Justifying lying still for two hours a week felt impossible until I finally tried one of Mel's masks.

"You did."

"I'd never steer you wrong."

"I'm sorry I ever doubted you."

"You are forgiven." She punctuates the last word by blowing a handful of glitter in my face. "Done."

"Finally," I choke out between coughs. But I'm grinning from ear to ear when Mel holds up a little compact mirror for me to see her handiwork. It's impossible not to be blown away by the stunning designs she's swirled all over my cheeks. They're ethereal yet menacing, like I'm a warrior princess about to grant you a wish right before ripping out your throat. "Wow."

"Thanks," she says, chuckling at my wide-eyed, gaped-mouth awe. She tucks paint brushes and sponges in the pockets of her art case. A glance at her watch has her picking up the pace. She fumbles a brush and takes a steadying breath before bending to pick it up.

It's not like that, indeed.

But I refuse to harass her about Everett. Not right now anyway. My focus should be on the game. Securing the win.

And grinding Hudson's face into the dirt.

"Hey, Leilani." Kendrick and the rest of my teammates huddle up around me. Each one wears the same colors smeared across their face in haphazard slashes and spots.

"Damn," Linda praises. "With the braids and the war paint, you look like a hot Viking."

"Yeah, very take-no-prisoners," Kendrick adds breathlessly.

"Thank you, guys."

Kendrick holds up a roll of paper. "Where do you want the banner?"

A mix of irritation and embarrassment buzzes through

my chest. My behavior in the Art Barn last night was child-ish; not exactly consistent with how a woman about to turn forty should act. Even if I'm at a summer camp that's meant to be nostalgic and make us feel like kids again.

And I hate to use him as an excuse, but Hudson knows exactly how to get under my skin. He burrows and pokes with his smug smirk and stupid hoodie. Who wears jeans and a sweatshirt in eighty-degree weather anyways? A sociopath, that's who. Someone capable of pushing me until I'm about to pop. Someone who drives me to act like a snarky little brat.

"Uh, Leilani?"

One glance at my team and I'm certain my inner mono-logue has played out all over my face. Thank fuck for the paint and glitter.

Kendrick wiggles the roll of paper again.

Right. The unfinished banner.

"Maybe we should scrap it this year." I hate to admit it, but perhaps being the bigger person is the best option. Espe-cially since we didn't get a chance to finish it.

"What? No. You worked so hard on it," Linda urges.

"But it's not even half—" The word *done* dries on my tongue as my teammates unroll the butcher paper and reveal a fully completed sign. *Hudson Sucks* spans the entire eight feet. When Mel and I scurried out of the Art Barn last night with our tails between—ok, fine—with *my* tail between *my* legs, the letters were barely outlined with only the first two filled in. But what my teammates hold is a fully formed banner complete with polka dots and zigzags for added flair.

I turn to Mel, who stands beside me in impressed shock. "Did you—"

"No," she cuts me off.

"Did you guys finish this?" I ask Kendrick and Linda. Both shake their heads.

"We assumed you went back after Hudson left and finished up," Linda says.

"Wasn't me." I mull it over and come to the only possible conclusion. I turn to Mel. "Can you thank Everett for me, please? He didn't have to do that. Not after how I behaved."

"You think he finished it?" my friend asks, checking her watch again.

"It's the only thing that makes sense."

"Not the only thing that makes sense. You know Hudson stayed behind to—"

"Thank Everett for me," I press more adamantly, because I'm not willing to accept her bizzarro alternate theory that my nemesis could have finished the project.

"Sure. Good luck today." She nudges my shoulder and takes off across the field.

Chapter Twelve

Hudson

I covertly watch as Leilani's team unrolls their banner—the one I completed last night after our hostile run-in. There's no way I can possibly hear the little surprised gasp she makes, but imagining it makes my ears tingle. And I swear her eyes actually sparkle as she takes in my effort. She looks to her friend Mel and then her teammates. Everyone shrugs. Not a single one of them knows it was me. Because why would I help my rival with something that directly pokes fun at me?

Because I'm whipped.

A simp.

That's what the kids are calling it, right? When you're so far gone for someone that you do secret little things to make them happy. Even when they'd sooner grind you beneath their boot than say thanks.

But that smile on her face. . .

I'd do the same thing ten times over.

"Yo, Hudson," my teammate Malik calls. "You with us, buddy?"

"He's distracted; too busy jerking his rage boner over Leilani," Jemma says, straight-faced and flat-toned.

Every other Tidal Wave member turns to Jemma. I have no clue if she notices their alarm or just doesn't give a fuck, because all she does is crack a few knuckles and watch me blankly. She's such a loose cannon. No, that's not quite right. A loose cannon is wild and unpredictable, flying around willy-nilly, leaving chaos in its wake. Jemma's calm, collected. Sinister. For a split second I'd considered a buddy system for this round but quickly dismissed the idea because I didn't want anyone to have to partner up with her. I'm pretty sure I'd be somewhat liable if shit went south, being team captain and all.

"I'm scoping out the competition." As I join my team, everyone loosens up a little. We go over the game plan discussed yesterday. "Is everyone clear on their roles?"

They all nod. It's not a complicated system. Malik and . . . shit, I forgot the other guy's name. Steve? Stuart? Whatever. Two of our guys will stay with our flag to play defense when the other team hits our home base. The rest of us will head into enemy territory and distract while, you guessed it, Jemma takes point. She's tiny, strong, and fast. The best shot we have is finding her an opening to snatch the flag and get it back to our side.

A shrill whistle pierces the muggy air.

Counselor Clark jogs to the middle of the field wearing his signature smears of zinc oxide and a black and white referee jersey that shows he might be taking this game as seriously as Leilani and I are.

"Huddle up, campers," he shouts as we converge on the boundary between our territories.

Leilani approaches and I'm blown away. From a distance, I could see that her face was covered in her team's colors. I assumed she looked pretty (because she always does). But up close?

Damn.

She's a goddess. A ruthless, colorful, warrior princess with arches of teal that emphasize her cheekbones and a dusting of glitter that highlights the rest of her splendor. Suddenly, I'm in high school again. A gangly dork obsessed with role-playing games and fantasy novels. Daydreaming about the Elvin Queen the DM sent to distract me so other players could take my gold.

I muse that a new kink has been unlocked, then realize it's only been revitalized.

Leilani Walker is precisely what adolescent me would have dreamed up in his hormone-fueled hallucination.

A drought rolls up my throat and dries my tongue.

I'm awestruck.

"Pratt," her agitated growl shakes me from the brink of collapse.

What's going on? Oh right. Capture the flag.

"Do you need a minute?" Clark asks with an edge of concern.

Glancing around, I see both teams are eyeing me with curiosity, except Jemma. Her face still says flat irritation.

"Nah, I'm good." My assurance comes out all croaky, but our counselor accepts it anyway.

"Cool. Cool. Then you all have five minutes to take your places and get ready. When I blow three times, that means we've started." He holds up a stopwatch and wails into his whistle once to announce our dismissal. "Get moving."

I turn but pause as Leilani's voice drifts sweetly on the stale afternoon heat. "Hey, Hudson."

"Yes?" What's it going to be? Eat shit? Fuck you? You suck?

Her eyes blaze, lips curling into a menacing sneer, but her voice is cotton candy sweet. "Good luck."

Why does that feel more threatening than anything else she could have said?

Chapter Thirteen

Leilani

The shrill triple whistle pierces the air, and mayhem ensues.

From my perch, I watch as Hudson's offensive line races forward. A few whoop and holler while others release *Braveheart*-worthy battle cries. Still others stealthily beeline for the playfield's side boundaries, like they think we aren't watching their useless attempts at covert maneuvers.

"Hold!" My bellow keeps my team at bay, even while some of the more antsy players pace like horses at the beginning of the Kentucky Derby. "Eyes on the edges."

We had originally agreed on a berserker-style attack but changed tactics last minute. Instead, the plan is to let as many of the enemies cross into our territory as possible. Then we corral and tag. If the bulk of the Tidal Wave players are frozen in a concentrated area, it'll take fewer players to guard them, thus freeing up more of ours to head across enemy lines.

I catch a glimpse of Hudson making his way down the field. He shouts a few words, but he must be using some kind of code, because it all sounds like word salad to me. Much of his team suddenly banks right.

"Cannonball lollipop! Cannonball *lollipop*! Not cannonball *roast beef*," he wails.

But it's too late; four of his teammates converge and cross the line. In an instant, four of mine surround them and tag each one.

"Sonofabitch," Hudson groans, diverting as quickly as possible away from the cluster of defense.

"I guess they got their roast beef and lollipops mixed up," Kendrick says with a low and rumbling laugh behind me.

"With a sophisticated code like that, I'm not surprised." I reach out and return his fist bump.

Eyes dart to where we stand and I give our team the go-ahead with an over-the-top thumb throat slice.

"Go get 'em, Cap. I can hold down the fort," Kendrick assures as he keeps tabs on Hudson and Jemma, who appear to be conferring far away from the frozen players.

"Protect her well, my friend."

I leap off the small platform that houses our flag and take off running directly down the middle of the field. The majority of the Tidal Waves are too preoccupied with freeing their captured teammates to even notice me whoosh by. Not to brag too much, but your girl's got speed. Between my long legs and sheer will to win, Usain Bolt can eat his heart out.

And with my attention so focused on the opposing team's flag, I can ignore the burn of my lungs, the sweat dripping down my back.

Fuck it's hot.

But I don't let it slow me down. Even when two of my opponents try to advance.

Patience. Wait…

They're within mere feet of me and I fake right before lunging left. One of them sees my dodge coming. But unfortunately for her, her buddy doesn't and slams right into her, taking them both to the dirt in a tangle of arms and legs and name-calling.

I never officially played football growing up, but all of my brothers did. And since there were so many of us kids, if I wanted attention, I had to toss myself into the fray of brotherly scrimmages. Let's just say I learned a thing or two, and capture the flag is always the best way to showcase the hard-earned agility.

The other team's platform looms up ahead with two Tidal Wave twats standing guard. A smirk pulls at my face because I know they don't stand a chance. Especially as I feel my teammates speeding up to flank me. We form a V with me at the apex.

"Draw them," I shout to the two on my left. They nod and peel off.

A flash of movement blurs to my right and I scan to see that Hudson is running parallel to our formation.

"Shit," I bark. To the two on my right, I shout, "Keep him busy, but be ready to guard me once I get the flag."

They dart off and do their best to tempt Hudson into trying to tag them, but it doesn't work. Apparently, all the *nanny-nanny-boo-boo-ing* they can muster isn't doing a damn thing to tear his focus from my advance. Frankly, I don't blame him. Our plan is pretty clear and my nemesis is quickly approaching. At this point all I can do is run faster.

Luckily, Linda and Albert have lured the two flag protectors into chasing them, leaving my target wide open. In some sort of adrenaline-feuled feat of strength, I bound up to the platform and get a fist of the orange flag.

Behind me, I hear the cheering and it makes me smile, but I haven't won yet. A team hasn't won until their opponent's flag is brought across the line of scrimmage.

"You're mine, Walker." The deep husk of Hudson's words scrape up my thighs, making them feel wobbly and useless.

"You wish it were true," I shoot back, frozen on the platform while I try to figure out exactly how to play this.

"You have no idea," he mutters low, and I'm not entirely convinced he meant to say it out loud.

I shove the flag down into the side pocket of my shorts; if I have any chance, it's with both hands free. Hudson tracks my movement with an almost hungry gaze.

Which gives me an idea.

A really, *really* bad one.

As his hands settle on the base of the platform, ready to heave up and tag me, I grip the bottom hem of my shirt and lift.

It does the trick. His hazel eyes darken with lust and he

zeroes in on my nipples. He's frozen, as are a couple of others in play nearby. As his eyes trail down to my newly pierced navel, I take advantage of his boob-induced paralysis and leap over him. The landing is hardly graceful—the last-minute decision to roll is the only reason I still have functioning knees.

While holstering my weapons, I scramble to my feet and haul ass across the midfield line.

The whistle blows, signaling the end of the game and our first win of the week. Kendrick descends from our platform and lopes over to me. He dips down, tucks his head between my thighs, and before I know what's happening, I'm perched on his massive shoulders while the rest of my team circles, shouting, "Hudson Sucks! Hudson Sucks!"

A few of the Tidal Wave members—clearly the less competitive ones—gather and offer words of congratulations.

Not Hudson, though.

He's still standing back at his platform. He scrubs a hand down his face before popping his hood up and striding off the field toward the guys' cabins.

Chapter Fourteen

Hudson

My low back tightens as I feel release mere pumps away. Lukewarm water sputters from the ancient showerhead onto my chest as I lean one arm against the tiled stall. Flashes of glimmering eyes swarm my head. Pink cheeks smeared with war paint and contorted in vicious determination. Perfect nipples pulled tight under my stare. I imagine what it would be like to slide into her mouth, nudge the back of her throat. I fist my cock harder, vigorously stroking myself with the cheap liquid soap available in the showers.

God, she's something else. An otherworldly, ethereal goddess manifesting as a warrior on the battlefield. I chuckle at these thoughts, fully aware of the effect these silly camp games have on me.

The effect Leilani Walker has on me.

My smile morphs into a grimace as I near the brink.

"Twelve minutes and thirty-three seconds. A new camp record. That's the third one I've broken since I started coming here."

I'm hallucinating. I must be because I hear Leilani's voice echo off the shower walls. Two sets of sandals slap in my direction.

"That's great and all, but, uh . . ." The other woman's voice trails off for a moment. "This is the men's shower."

"So?"

I maintain my grip but slow my strokes. Listening.

"Someone's already in here. Probably a guy too."

"*So?*" Leilani repeats with more emphasis.

"I can't shower with a bunch of men."

"Mel, no one's asking you to do a group shower scene. Then again, you missed out on so much by being married for seventeen years. Maybe it's time to sow your wild oats or whatever."

"No one's sowing anything."

"The smears of paint all over your body say otherwise." A loud crack snaps through the air, followed by Leilani's yelp. "What the hell?"

"Cheeky brat."

"What's with the sudden spanking? Did you pick up a second job as a dominatrix?"

Fuck, now I'm thinking about getting *my* hands on Leilani's tight ass too. Bending her over a log in the woods during the moonlit multi-flag capture event. Landing my palm on her bare cheeks, frayed jean shorts tangled around her ankles so she can't sidestep the strikes.

My erection throbs in my hand and a low moan slips from my lips into the steamy air.

"Yep. I'm out," Melody all but shouts, flip-flops slapping her heels as she scurries out of the shower.

"Mel, wait," Leilani calls after her friend then lets out a resigned huff. "Who's in here?"

Right. Like I'd answer and reveal that it's me in the stall, naked . . . masturbating.

Her sandals squelch along the soggy floor in my direction. It's not like she has to *try* to find me, there are about ten stalls lined up with plastic curtains that barely span the width of each doorway. And there's only one showerhead on, so her target is easily identifiable.

Still, her advance spikes my blood like top-shelf liquor. I'm drunk on her possible reactions to finding me. There's no quieting the pulsing arousal and pressure in my sack. I'm wound tight from competing against this woman. Horny as fuck, and her closing in on my solo shower sesh is ratcheting up the thrill of being caught.

By her.

"I said, who?" Her feet are visible beneath the flimsy curtain. I can see the glossy lavender coating on her nails and a delicate gold toe ring on her right foot.

I don't answer. Thinking that if I ignore her, she'll go away.

Deep down, I'm hoping she won't.

"If you don't fess up"—her fingers curl around the edge of the curtain—"I'll see for myself."

She's playing a game of chicken while I choke mine.

My heart's a battering ram against my chest, trying its damnedest to bust through my ribs. The breath I hold in my lungs isn't the only thing that aches to be released. Until finally her hand drops away and I feel an intense surge of disappointment. I turn back to the showerhead, aiming to finish what I started, when the scrape of rusty metal rings drags across an equally wrecked shower rod.

I glance over my shoulder and there she is. Still paint-smeared and dusty from the game, even though it's been hours since her victory. One hand pops to her hip. She's wearing those frayed cut-off shorts that I keep fantasizing about; white strings dangling, tickling the soft, tan skin of her impossibly long legs. A bratty smirk tips her lips until it drops away.

I could play this so many different ways. First instinct is to tell her to buzz off then reach back and whip the curtain closed. Second instinct? Pull her into the spray. Or I could make a flirty quip about getting an eyeful.

None of those options feel quite right, though.

"Hudson." Her lips part on a gasp, and her pupils expand so fast they obliterate the golden flare of her eyes. She rakes her gaze down my back, to my ass and then back up. When they settle on mine, she inadvertently licks her lips. I watch the pink tip hit the corner of her mouth. Imagine she drops to her knees and takes me whole. "Sorry. I—I didn't mean to barge—"

"Are you?" I interrupt her ramble before it gets going.

"Am I what?" Her voice isn't timid. Leilani Walker is

incapable of being timid. There's more of that challenge in her tone that I love so much.

"Are you *sorry*?"

She scoffs huskily. "Not particularly."

It's impossible to tell if she's pleased with what she sees or is basking in the triumph of my shame and embarrassment.

However, I'm not embarrassed in the least.

"I figured you wouldn't be. If you'll excuse me, I'm kind of in the middle of something." Returning my gaze to the back of the stall isn't easy. My eyes compulsively seek this woman at all times. And with stakes like these, it takes a mighty control I didn't know I possessed to look away.

Only, she still doesn't leave.

"Walker," I warn.

"Yes, Pratt," she replies with forced sweetness.

"Policing me? Shouldn't I be granted *some* privacy?"

"It's a public space."

She's not going anywhere, that much is clear. Which means I need to diffuse my . . . situation. I prepare to launch into the typical train of thought that cools me off in inconvenient scenarios, but I decide against it. I was here first. She knows what I'm doing. She could leave at any time.

And yet she doesn't.

So, I turn.

Facing her now, I capture her eyes with mine, arch a brow, and slowly travel the length of my aching cock. Down to the base and back to the tip. The crinkle of the plastic shower curtain is obscene under her grip, as is her breathing, which gradually speeds up. I glance down at myself, welcoming her to do the same.

And when she does . . . when she lets that little gasp tumble from her perfect lips, I increase my speed. Tighten my hold so it's nearly unbearable. The point of no return quickens and I stroke in time to the erratic beat of my wild heart.

She bites her lower lip, drags those perfectly white teeth over the pillowy softness that would feel incredible stretched around me.

Suddenly, I'm coming. Triggered by her presence, and sweaty, dirt-smeared skin, and blown-out pupils. She looks up to me again as shudders rack down my spine. Water trickles over my heaving shoulders and washes my spend down the drain. My breathing slows.

Leilani hasn't said anything. Her eyes continue to dart all over me in a way I can almost feel. A flush has bloomed from her chest up the length of her elegant neck. I think of how warm and soft the skin there would be beneath my fingertips.

I've been desired by women before. It's not cockiness. It's simply a fact that I am the type of man many people find attractive. But this woman doesn't seem like she merely desires me.

She wants to devour me.

The notion jets a fresh wave of lust through me. If I weren't so exhausted from the events of the day—wrecked from her watching me while I pleasure myself—I'd probably be hard again in a matter of minutes.

But suddenly, something clicks inside of her.

She shakes herself out of a lusty stupor, blinking like she just returned to her body, and smiles wanly at me. Her voice is hoarse. "Thanks for the show."

I huff out a weak laugh, taking the opportunity to soap and rinse before shutting off the shower and reaching for my beach towel.

"Anytime, Walker." And she has no idea how fucking much I mean it.

Right as I wrap the towel around my hips, she steps back and enters the stall next to mine.

"How's the water pressure?" she asks with forced casualness, pulling her curtain closed.

"Unsatisfying," I offer, hoping she catches my double meaning. That voyeurism moment was erotic, but left me wanting. Something tells me she feels similarly.

She hums noncommittally and turns on the water.

After gathering my things, I pause outside her curtain until she says, "Not a chance, Pratt."

I shake my head and exit the men's shower, chuckling the whole way.

Chapter Fifteen

Leilani

"You watched him?" Melody chokes on her beer, sputtering a mouthful all over herself.

"I did." I hand her the napkin I had wrapped around my plastic cup so she can dab away the drops trailing down her cleavage.

I'm perched on the railing of the deck of our cabin while a party rages inside. By raging, I mean everyone's tearing into a case of Rainier tallboys to make the karaoke sound better. Mel leans both elbows on the weathered wood beside me and looks out over the patchy lawn, where a few campers are playing cornhole.

"As he pleasured himself . . ." Her shock is cute. She's not a prude, but for whatever reason this is short-circuiting her brain.

"Correct."

"That must have been something," Mel muses, successfully swallows down a gulp of beer, and then turns to face me.

What went down between Hudson and me this afternoon was unexpected. Before I knew it was him in the shower, I wasn't in love with the idea that someone was diddling themselves while we were in there. So, I figured I'd shame the culprit and move it along. What I didn't anticipate was how much finding him in that state would affect me.

Nor did I anticipate the body he's been hiding beneath those damned hoodies. Who knew he'd have cords of muscle lining his back? Or tree trunk legs? And that bubble butt?

The business bro is ripped.

Seems like a crime to hide all that under some drab, baggy sweatshirt.

"I didn't hate it." I giggle then clear my throat to cover the ridiculous sound. I can't be giggling over Hudson freaking Pratt.

"Anything beyond that happen?" Suspicion taints her words while her laser beam eyes bore into the side of my head.

"I said thanks and then took a shower."

"*With him*?" I'd forgotten how high my friend's voice could go. Dogs a mile away are probably howling at the shriek.

I laugh and gently nudge her with my elbow. "Alone, Mel. I took a shower alone."

"Wow. I'm surprised."

I shrug in response.

Franky, I kinda am too. Did I want to invite Hudson into my stall to fool around? Maybe. But I wouldn't confess that to her, let alone to Hudson. Not a chance. I'll admit, my brain did a momentary record scratch when I saw what he's working with.

"Legendary," Mel sighs wistfully.

A burst of laughter fills the cabin. One butchered song ends and another begins.

"Your turn to spill the beans," I demand, cringing slightly at the off-key caterwauling coming from inside.

Her ears flame. "There aren't any beans to spill," she insists.

Of the three of us, Mel's always been the steel trap of the group. It's practically impossible to get anything out of her. Ever. Which is why her divorce came as such a shock when she finally told us. We had no clue that she and Lance were struggling. And while she never really sang his praises, she spent even less time airing his dirty laundry.

"You've been spending an awful lot of time in the Art Barn."

She darts her eyes away and takes a long pull of beer.

Evasive harlot.

A shuffle of feet and blend of masculine voices float on the warm night air toward us on the path from the guys' cabins.

"We come bearing booze," Charles's voice cuts through the darkness.

The cluster of men approach the steps, each one carrying a different fifth of some kind of alcohol.

"Saved by the panty raid," Mel mumbles under her breath.

The Hump Day Panty Raid is a long-held, though unsanctioned, camp tradition. The guys bring the liquor and women bring a pair of panties to trade. Archaic? Most definitely. So much so that one year, the girls demanded the guys provide the undies for once, but the swap was short-lived and quickly regretted. None of us wanted to touch the worn boxers and tighty-whities brought as offerings. It's much better the original way. I participate even though I stick to beer. But it's all in good fun and hard not to get wrapped up in the silliness of the custom.

A few of the new arrivals don't stop and chat with Mel or me and bound up the steps. We all wince at the abysmal rendition of "My Heart Will Go On" blaring through the door as the rest of the guys file inside. Charles hangs back with an aloof Hudson standing behind him.

"Hey, fellas. Nice night, huh?" My friend is all too thrilled with the interruption, but I eye her sternly and try to convey to her telepathically that I won't be dropping the whole Everett thing.

"Perfect for a starlit stroll, don't you think?" Charles asks.

"Yeah, I could go for a—" I begin until he interrupts me by pressing a bottle of Malibu in my hands.

"I was talking to Mel." He turns to her, extends a hand, and raises his brows. "Walk to the lake with me?"

She beams happily as he pulls her beside him. "I'd love to. Bye, Leilani. *Hudson.* Try to keep it in your pants, will ya?"

"Since I'm not in a shower, that shouldn't be an issue," he retorts levelly.

Charles and Mel head down the trail toward the lake laughing and chattering away like they've known each other for years. Once out of sight, my shower pal turns to me.

"What's with that?" I ask, gesturing to the backs of our friends as they disappear down the path.

"He thinks we should talk," Hudson says.

I roll my eyes but don't say anything. As far as I'm concerned, there's nothing to discuss. We had a moment and that moment's passed. I set the fifth Charles handed me on the porch.

"Mind if I sit?"

"Depends on what you brought for me." When his brows scrunch in confusion, I nod to the bottle he's holding. Understanding dawns, and he passes me the booze. "Single malt? A little classy for summer camp."

He hops up and sits when I pat the railing to welcome him aboard.

"It's all I had left in my cabinet." He shrugs. "It's a little dusty, but should be fine."

There's a physical static pulsing in the space between us. Even though we aren't touching, I can feel the denim of his pants on my freshly shaved legs. He shoves both hands into his hoodie pockets and bobs his knee.

"So," he begins, but doesn't say anything more.

"Oh, Jesus, Pratt." I'm over this immature awkwardness. We're adults, for fuck's sake. I deposit the Scotch next to the Malibu at my feet and turn to him. "There's nothing to discuss. I watched you masturbate in the shower. It doesn't change anything."

"You don't think so?" It's tough for me to decipher his tone. Like he's trying to cling to this aloof vibe, but a waiver of disappointment curls the edges of his words.

"Look." I turn to him and my knee brushes against his. He tenses and I quickly readjust so we have a bit of space between us. "This is, what? Your fifth summer here too, right?" He nods and I continue. "People hook up here all the time—not that that's what we did—but it's no shock that one of us finally saw the other a la nude. Everyone calls this place Camp Clandestine, remember? All kinds of sex-adjacent things go down here. What happened in the shower . . . It didn't really mean anything."

Hudson's chin dips to his chest, that knee of his still bouncing wildly. His silence is unnerving. Does he wish it meant something? I want to ask, but what would I do with the information if he said yes? Kiss him? Flirt? Get my hands all over his secretly hot bod?

Ridiculous.

"So now what?" he asks. I still can't read him.

"The way I figure it, we have two options."

The side of his mouth quirks. With the stubble and the cabin's porch light hitting him just right, he's sexy. I'm surprised I never noticed it before now. Fine. I did notice it in years past, but I'm loosened up with beer and the memory of him gripping his dick, so I'm actually willing to admit it right now.

"And they are?"

"We head in and keep our distance or you congratulate me on an incredible victory and spend a little time gushing over how awesome I was."

The low rumble of his laugh wraps around me like a hug. What would an embrace from this man feel like?

"You were impressive, Leilani," he admits.

My chuckle mingles with his. "Are you referring to my victory or when I flashed you?"

"Oh, the boobs, definitely. What?" He responds to the judgy look I have on my face. "I do believe you lifted your shirt of your own accord. I just stood there and enjoyed it."

There's no denying it. It was a strategy and it paid off. "Fair. Please continue with the praise."

"I never assumed that would be your kink." He captures my gaze with his.

"It's not." The heat still manages to climb up my neck and light my cheeks on fire as I think about him calling me a good girl like they do in some of my favorite romance novels. "I happen to believe—on a purely platonic level—that singing someone's praises when they do something spectacular is the right thing to do."

"Spectacular, huh?"

"You heard me." I take a long gulp of my beer and pretend I don't feel his eyes take a leisurely stroll down the length of me.

"Fine. Never was there a more impressive victory than the history that we all witnessed today on that capture the flag field. You will live in infamy, and may we forever remember the cunning and boldness that is Leilani Walker."

"I couldn't have said it better if I tried," I say with a puffed chest and raised chin. But my cheeks are aflame with the almost sincerity of his tone. I have to get a little distance to clear my swirling head. My bare feet hit the creaky boards and I back toward the door. "Heading in for more beer."

"What do you think about upping the ante of our wager?" There's seduction in the caramel depths of his question.

''No'' is the correct answer to this potentially dangerous game.

"Sure," I say instead.

"If I win the next two games," Hudson hops off the railing and stalks close to me. Before I know it, we're toe to toe, his sneakers barely touching my bare feet. Bracing his forearm on the top of the doorframe, he leans over me. Caging me in as my back presses against the scratchy wood. I can smell his woodsy-citrusy scent, and memories of him in the shower, muscles flexing as he orgasms, flash through my mind with lethal potency. "You let me take you on a date when camp is over."

For a moment—the briefest, blink of a second—I consider how much pleasure seeing this man in the real world would bring me. What it might be like to dress up for him. The gentle pressure of his hand on the small of my back as he leads me through a crowd. The taste of his lips as he kisses me goodnight.

Then just as fast, reality takes hold and the niggling voice snarling at the back of my subconscious elbows her way to the front.

Hudson Pratt is exactly the type of man that I absolutely loathe. A douchebag who values money over people. Someone so focused on climbing his ladder with no qualms about who or how many people he has to stomp down in the process. Someone who gets what they want when they want it and raises hell when something doesn't go their way. He's selfish, egotistical, and calculating. Nope. People like that have already affected my life in irreparable ways. I've dated his kind—almost *married* that type of man—and I'd be a fool to welcome it across my threshold again.

But since I have no intention of letting him win, I agree to play along. Because seeing him lose and miss out on something he wants is too good to pass up.

"Fine," I say, lifting my chin in defiance. "But when I win—"

"*If* you win, then what?" His chin dips and I wonder if he's seeking permission to lean in for a kiss.

"*When* I win"—I grab a fistful of the front of his sweatshirt—"on top of losing your precious hoodies for a full year . . . this will be your last summer at Camp Clandestine. You won't be able to return ever again."

Chapter Sixteen

Hudson

Another Hump Day Panty Raid comes to an end. Multiple campers have paired, or grouped, and snuck off to screw in the woods surrounding the girls' cabins. Two dudes—looks like it might be the quitters Brad and Chad from Leilani's team—sprawl in the grass next to pools of their own vomit. And a die-hard Missy Elliott fan (*cough, cough,* Charles) belts out a slurred version of "Get Ur Freak On."

A minute ago, I bid my crooning friend farewell. Today was a big, exhausting day, and I'm beat. Plus, if there's any hope of defeating Leilani at the next two games, I'd better get some rest while I can.

When I win . . . this will be your last year at Camp Clandestine.

My head still spins at her stakes. Banning me from camp is a bold move, one that would be hard to come to terms with. But her agreeing to *my* terms somehow makes the risk worth it. I still can't believe that I had the balls to propose the date. We've had this camp enemies thing going since we met four years ago, but to be honest, the sentiment eventually became one-sided. The gradually developing crush I've harbored for this woman has reached intoxicating levels. It didn't hit me until after my third year here what the rivalry we shared was doing to me. But even as my intrigue grew, I never made a move. Mostly because my attention was focused elsewhere.

The higher I climbed on the corporate ladder, the more my work consumed me. The more *success* consumed me. And while I quickly learned to disconnect here at camp, the second I'd step back into reality, my neglected responsibilities would blast me in the face. Typically, once I returned home from camp, I'd spend the remainder of the weekend fielding emails, panicked voicemails, Slack messages, and once even received a subpoena. What they say about there being no rest for the wicked is accurate; I can attest to that.

But now things are different.

Now, I'm adrift. The same aimlessness that would have given me a *figurative* heart attack in my heyday now has me on my way to a healthier version of myself. Physically and mentally.

The social media marketing business I devoted my life to for the last seven years—one that consistently pulls in nine figures of revenue each year—is no longer my concern. The high-maintenance clients I played butler, bitch, and whipping boy to are *no longer* my concern. And in between those chilling slashes of dread that occasionally climb my spine, I've been experiencing a novel sense of calm. A sensation foreign to me since, well . . .

Forever.

So now, I have nothing *but* time to make a play for Leilani.

I should have point-blank asked her out. Acted like a grown man and went for it. But I worried that if I didn't hide behind the safety of a childish wager, she'd mistake my sincerity for vulnerability. Or worse, she'd assume I was fucking with her. Playing a mind game to throw her off so I could be the victor this year. Putting higher stakes to our usual competition feels safer. Even if I risk losing the one week per year where I get to bask in the glow that is Leilani Walker.

Which means I can't lose.

A massive yawn creeps up and motivates me to head back to my cabin. My bunk is calling and I must go. As I make my way, my checked skate shoes crunching the twigs and gravel, I hear the cabin door I recently exited creak open.

"Heading to the showers again so you can bash the bishop?" The seductive cadence of Leilani's voice warms me, but it's her words that halt my steps.

"Bash the bishop?" I turn to her as she strolls forward. Her sneakers are untied, which means she must have thrown them on in haste in order to catch up to me. It's impossible to keep my lips from pulling up in a smile at the implication.

"You know," she shrugs, revealing a mouth-watering strip of tanned midriff. "Choke the chicken. Beat your meat. Pull your pud."

"No, I get it, I've just never heard it put that way. But to answer your question, no. I'm off to get some sleep. There's a wager to win."

She nods, stuffs her hands into the pockets that poke out the bottom of those tiny cut-off shorts she always wears. The toe of her sneakers drags a semicircle in the sparse gravel.

"Unless there's a reason for me to stay," I risk.

Leilani huffs a gentle laugh but doesn't turn me down. Instead, she steps closer, so close that I can smell the single malt scotch on her breath. It doesn't escape me that she drank what I brought to the party. She pulls her hand from her pocket and I notice there's something clenched in her fingers, but in the dwindling light of the campfire a few yards away I can't make it out.

"No. You should get some rest." She reaches out and slips her fist into the pocket of my hoodie, depositing whatever she'd been holding.

I reach for her, but she slips away before I have the chance to find purchase.

I'd be a fool not to watch her go. After I've enjoyed my fill of her long legs, perky ass, and flowing raven hair, I reach into my pocket to see what she left me. My fingers twine around soft lace and elastic, and a jolt of lust shakes away my fatigue.

Panties.

Her panties.

The bit of midnight blue fabric dangles from my fingers and I have to resist the urge to see if it smells like her.

"For luck," she calls from the porch right before stepping into the cabin. "Cuz you're gonna need it."

Chapter Seventeen

Second Year of Camp: Hudson

I'm a risk-taker. Haven't always been, but over the last few years, I've learned to throw caution to the wind and go on pure, predatory instinct. On occasion, I've bowed out of a deal or project because it was a fool's errand. But I've also honed my skills to recognize when doubling down is the only option.

Coming back to camp this year was one of those moments.

I almost didn't. Last summer, I told Charles and Eddie on the way home from camp that I didn't ever want to go back. That it was a complete waste of time, and the next guys' trip better be to Vegas or some other party spot.

But as the months ticked by, Camp Clandetine kept invading my thoughts. Something nagged at me from the back of my brain. Like a song whose melody you hum incessantly but can't quite remember the words to. Or like you're forgetting something important that didn't make it on your to-do list.

Or, more accurately, like unfinished business.

I hated losing to Leilani.

I hated watching her throw my phones into that fucking lake.

But most of all, I hated the idea of leaving off on a note of humiliation.

I knew that if I swallowed my pride and went back for vengeance, I'd come out on top. She wouldn't be able to beat me again. It would be her phones I'd be hurling into the lake —metaphorically speaking, because I'd have a completely different *reward* in mind. The conviction swirled around and around my thoughts until the hypothetical fantasy just wasn't enough.

Charles and Eddie were both shocked when I hopped into our group chat and told them I wanted to go back to camp with them.

CHARLES

You sure, man? You hated it last year.

EDWARD

Yeah. You told us, like, forty times on the drive home.

HUDSON

I hated LOSING.

But that won't be a problem this time.

CHARLES

Why not?

HUDSON

Simple. I'll just win.

CHARLES

ROFL 🤣

HUDSON

What?

CHARLES

That simple, huh?

HUDSON

Yes.

CHARLES

She tasted blood.

I doubt she'd give up victory that easily.

HUDSON

Not a problem. I'm determined. Focused.

I refuse to let Leilani beat me.

If she's even there this year.

EDWARD

One sec . . .

Bianca says she will be.

HUDSON

There. It's settled.

CHARLES

Alright, man. I'll add you to the
registration so you end up in the same
cabin as Eddie and me.

HUDSON

Let me know what I owe you.

CHARLES

You got it.

"To all my doubters," I crow into the microphone I'm clenching while standing on the mess hall deck. I pointedly mean mug both of my buddies. "You said I didn't have a chance. Well, guess what? I knew I'd win. I *decided* I'd win. And look where I am."

"Bragging about winning a silly camp game?" Leilani grumbles from beside me. What a spoilsport. The amount of gloating she did last year is still fresh in my mind. There's no way I'm letting her off without subjecting her to at least the same level of mockery that she inflicted on me.

I'm sure my smile is sinister as I turn to face her. "Any last words?"

She crosses her arms and pops out a denim-clad hip. White pockets stick out the bottom of the frayed edges and mingle with a few dangly white strings. She taps her foot impatiently, and I inadvertently trail my eyes down the length of her long, tan legs. Stunning legs. I'm shocked I didn't realize how sexy they were last year. Though I suppose I was more focused on the mission and less so on the physical attributes of my enemy. But now that I'm really looking at her, she has the kind of legs I'd love to have wrapped around my waist, or better yet, my head—

"Hudson," Leilani gripes. "Can we get the fuck on with it?"

My mouth is dry. I'm suddenly wishing I could drink some of the ice water from either of the two orange coolers sitting beside me. But every drop I take for myself is one drop less available for payback.

The managing counselor, Astrid, steps up beside me and reaches out a hand. "Uh, let me hold that for you. These mics are sort of expensive."

I smile sweetly at the cheery redhead and hand over the equipment then settle one hand on each handle of one of the jugs we use to refill our water bottles. The ice water sloshes around as I strut over to my nemesis. She keeps eye contact, as though doing so were some sort of act of defiance.

Fine by me. Seeing the reaction on her face will be priceless. It wouldn't be as fun if she turned away.

"You ready for this?" I ask.

She tightens her arms around her chest and growls. "Do it already."

I grin, happy to oblige, and lift the heavy container above our heads. It takes some effort but as I tip it over and pour the frigid water all over Leilani, the horrified squeal she lets out makes it all worth it.

"Holy fuck! Ohmygod that's fucking cold." She's shrieking and cursing loudly, and I watch with unadulterated glee.

Leilani Walker is an absolute vision. Drenched from head

to toe, her hair is plastered down the sides of her face, arms, and back. Those little shorts of hers stuck to her goose bumped skin. And I am silently thanking whatever deity that might exist for compelling her to wear a white T-shirt for the closing ceremonies. It clings to her curvy form. And I drink in of the sight of her nipples poking through the fabric as she shivers.

I'd almost describe my reaction to her as lust . . . if I didn't loathe her so much.

The jug hangs from one of my hands and I hold the other out to Astrid to take back the microphone.

"We're not done yet, princess. You remember what you need to say, right?" I croon, eyebrow arched, loving every second of this situation.

She nods, and I hold out the mic to her mouth.

Shit. If looks could kill, I'd be a pile of ash because the fire in Leilani's golden-brown eyes is incendiary. But still, she does as she agreed to and leans forward.

"Please, sir," she says through gritted teeth. I'm unsure if she's clenching them in rage or to keep them from chattering. "May I have another?"

"Why of course you may."

I hand the microphone back to Astrid and trade out the empty orange water cooler for the full one beside me. As I approach her, I grin wickedly.

And to think. I almost missed out on this by not coming to camp this year.

I vow to come back again.

Year after year, I plan to return.
If for no other reason than to best Lailani Walker.

Chapter Eighteen

Thursday Morning: Leilani

"Hey, watch it."

I slick my hair back over my head after cresting the surface of Heartbreak Lake, and cringe apologetically at Bianca, whom I accidentally splashed with my not-so-graceful dive attempt.

"My bad," I say, doggie paddling in her direction. "Guess my skills have lapsed since college."

"Wait, that was intentional?" she teases, swiping a couple of drops from the cover of her book and readjusting on her floaty. "I thought you fell in."

The temptation to flip her into the murky depths beckons, but I'd hate to ruin the novel I'm letting her borrow. Mel and I were shocked when our elusive friend strolled into the cabin this morning right as the two of us

110

were about to head to morning swim. Bianca looked a little befuddled, if dazed, but ultimately agreed to join us when we invited her along. So far she hasn't clued us in on why she's here and not getting railed by Eddie. All we've gotten from her was a clipped comment about "coming up for air" followed by a change in topic.

"I'll have you know I was the second-best high diver on the team my sophomore year."

"And you would have been first if someone hadn't switched your suit with one that was two sizes smaller," Bianca and Mel both recite like they've heard me lament that very complaint often, which they have.

"Hey. You'd have a hard time executing a reverse three-and-a-half somersault in a pike position too if you had a wedgie crammed so far up your ass that black spots were peppering your vision."

My friends chuckle and it's impossible not to join in. I'm so happy to be spending the morning with both of them in my favorite place at camp. You'd think on the field for capture the flag would be the top for me, but while I live for the competition, I find my peace here on the lake. She's not the prettiest or the clearest, but facing east the little bay warms nicely under the rising sun. I'm hopeless to resist taking a dip every morning that I'm here. When I'm back home or at work having a rough day, I often find myself daydreaming about jumping off the dock and swimming to the buoy in the center. Away from my troubles, bobbing on the gentle laps and ripples while I look up to the clear blue sky and count the whisps of white hanging there. Sometimes, I even imagine I'll hear ringing bubbling up from where Hudson's phones now reside. The watery chirps would mingle with the gently rustling leaves of the surrounding trees and croaking frogs that live around the water's edge.

"How was the panty raid last night?" Bianca asks as she turns her attention back to the water-speckled paperback she's holding.

I wait for Mel to respond, but she floats on her back instead, pretending not to hear the question.

"She pulled a *you*," I finally contribute when the silence has stretched a bit too long. "Charles dragged her to the lake for a walk then came back without her a couple hours later, explaining that she was in capable hands."

Bianca looks up from her pages with an expression of equal parts pride and shock. "Where'd you go last night, Mel?"

She doesn't respond, still floating on her back a few feet away. Her eyes closed as she slowly swipes her fingers through the water out to her side.

"She can't hear you," I say.

"Oh, she can freaking hear me. Mel. *Mel*." Bianca looks around, presumably for a place to set her paperback. When she can't find one, she huffs indignantly and turns to me. "Splash her for me, will ya?"

I roll my eyes but do as she asks, first sending little droplets her way then upgrading to a deluge she can no longer ignore until her butt sinks and she jackknifes to a stand.

"Whaaat?" she bemoans, giving us a glimpse of the irritated parent version of her that's about ready to burst from another round of *hey mom, guess what?*

"Where did you go last night?" Bianca tries again, lifting her sunglasses, and regards Mel with her patented laser-beams-of-truth. If anyone can get anything out of our tight-lipped friend, it's Bee.

"I went for a walk with Charles. We were missing our kids and spent most of the time talking about them."

"That's all you talked about? The conversation didn't veer to a certain art teacher you happen to find positively lickable?" I press. I'm not convinced she didn't confide in Charles. He's exactly the type you talk to about the hard stuff. First of all, the guy's a detective. Literally. He'd gotten the promotion right before coming to camp four years ago when I met him. Since then, I've been on the receiving end of his moments of silence designed to keep someone talking on a number of occasions. Besides that, he's got this calm and warm demeanor. He's naturally disarming.

"That's all we talked about," Mel doubles down. I'm still not convinced and eye her with as much scrutiny as I can muster. Bianca must do the same because eventually Mel blurts out something to throw the focus off of her. "Leilani flashed Hudson yesterday. And saw him naked. Oh, and gave him her panties!"

"How do you know that last one?" She wasn't even with us for the entire night. It wasn't until we coaxed Charles to give us the karaoke mic and tucked him into Bianca's rarely used bunk that Mel came sauntering in with wet hair and a few lingering smears of paint on her skin.

"I'm a mom," she grins like the Cheshire Cat. "I see everything."

"Hopefully not everything," Bianca mumbles with a nervous chuckle. Then she turns to me. "Spill."

Resistance is futile, so instead of denying, I give the abridged version. "Hudson and I raised the stakes of our capture the flag wager."

"And this involved nudity and your underpants, how?" Bianca asks, gesturing with her hand that she requires more context.

Processing what went down last night hasn't quite happened yet. It was almost too much piled on top of watching him masturbate in the shower before that. And flashing him at the first CTF game.

A lot happened yesterday.

New and *confusing* things.

"If I win, Hudson can't come back to camp," I say, peering at my feet as they sink into the silt. The ripple of lake water distorts my legs, making them appear wobbly in a way that matches how they actually feel when I think of never seeing that infuriating man again.

Would camp even be worth attending if I didn't have a nemesis to come back to? I could still compete in the CTF tournament, but it's impossible to predict whether it would light my fire the same way without our rivalry.

Except I *know* it wouldn't be the same.

I expect scolding, chastising, hell, maybe even a shocked

chuckle. But the complete silence coming from my friends unnerves me. Their wide-eyed expressions take me aback.

Did I force him to put too much on the line? He could have said no. Could have demanded I adjust my stakes, but he didn't. Which means he is either fully convinced he'll win or he recognizes this bet for what it is.

A true, last-ditch effort.

"And if he wins?" Mel interrupts my mile-a-minute thoughts.

My lower lip tingles where I bite it. "I have to go out with him after camp's over."

"Like on a *date*?" Bianca shrieks. I flinch as she fumbles my book and nearly drops it into the lake.

"Will you be careful with that?" I gingerly tug the book from her hands, pinching the spine between my forefinger and thumb. After wading back to the shore, I wrap the novel —which I'd hate to see destroyed because I haven't had a chance to read it yet—safely in my towel. Instead of splashing back into the lake, I pad my way along the dock to where my friends are floating. I sit on the edge with my feet dangling into the cool water. "Yes, like a date."

"Finally," Bianca shouts, her inflatable slice of watermelon makes that sticky plastic sound as she dramatically flops back onto it. "I haven't been able to figure out what's wrong with you two."

"What's that supposed to mean?"

Bianca grins. "You've been playing this will-they-won't-they bullshit for years, when we all see plain as day that you have a thing for each other."

"Wrong. Hudson's hot, I'll give you that, but he is the last guy I'd ever be into."

"Um," Mel raises her hand to interrupt Bianca and me going at each other. "Why wouldn't you be into him? I mean, you say he's your enemy and all, but I don't think you've ever given me the reasons for the clash."

"Because he stands for everything I hate." Even as I aim for calm, I feel the sneer pull at my lips to reveal my incisors. That man makes me feel feral when I think about our first meeting, though I think right now, some of my rage is directed inward for enjoying our interactions so much this week. For lusting after another glimpse of my rival, naked in the shower. Guilt weasels its way in and makes itself at home.

I'm betraying myself.

Specifically, the four-years-ago version who swore she'd never fall for a man like that again.

"It's just a job, Leilani. And Hudson isn't Mike." Bianca's voice has softened. She and Melody know all about my ex-fiancé. How he prioritized work over me every single time. How when I told him I was done, he proposed anyway, making all these promises about how he'd change. I'd clung to our history together. When we met, he was so sweet. So attentive. With Mike, I felt special . . . singular. A sensation that's wildly difficult to feel when you grow up with four brothers and a sister. Especially when both of your parents work. My mom and dad did their best. I know they love me and my siblings, but contending with so many kids? Let's just say attention was in short supply.

Which was why being the center of Mike's universe was so intoxicating.

Until I wasn't anymore.

The worst part was making a fool of myself by sticking around for so long in hopes that he'd change. Which he never did. So I vowed to protect my time instead of wasting it on anyone promising to be better. It's not that I believe people don't *want* to change.

It's that they are incapable of it.

For whatever reason, neither of my friends understands my loathing of Hudson, nor my inability to separate the current version of him from the douchey first impression four years ago. So, I aim to clarify it for them.

"Bee, would you date a dentist?" I ask.

She cringes and absently drapes a hand across her lips. "Not even to save your life," she says through her fingers.

"Blunt, but also, see?"

"But that's because I have a phobia." She glances at Mel, who's staring quizzically at us both. "Traumatic experience when I was fifteen. Novocain wore off and I could feel everything." She turns back to me and shudders. "I have history."

"And I don't?"

"With Mike, sure. Not with Hudson."

"They're one and the same." By this point, I'm ready to be done with this conversation. I get that it's hard to explain. But the last thing I want is to wake up each morning, roll over, and wonder if my partner will choose me that day. "Hudson and I would never work. We're oil and water, so even if he does win—fairly, this time—it won't go past that one date. It's a waste of time for us both."

"Then what's your plan?" Mel asks. I don't think she's blinked for the last few minutes, she's so enraptured with this conversation.

"Easy," I say with forced nonchalance that I'll hopefully believe myself. "All I have to do is win."

Chapter Nineteen

Hudson

Sleep was not a thing last night. Not for me anyway. After stumbling away from cabin number six with Leilani's sexy little panties gripped in my fist, I ignored my mind's protests to go after her and went straight to bed. I may have managed a few winks, but it's more likely that the images of her playing through my head were sweaty daydreams rather than actual shut-eye.

I'm still feeling the insomnia and it's already well into the afternoon.

The final splash of coffee in my compostable cup is ice cold. Not because it took me forever to drink it but because I kept going back all day for refills long after the carafe's warming plate switched off. By my count, I've had more than two full pots to myself. The caffeine vibrations are likely the only thing keeping me upright at the moment. That and the chance that I might win our little bet and finally spend some time with the woman of my dreams outside of camp. Worst case, I lose and never get to see her again.

For luck. Cuz you're gonna need it.

Leilani's not wrong. With how depleted I feel, it's going to take some hidden store of energy I have yet to tap into to beat her.

"You look like shit, dude," Lex—or perhaps it's Luthor, one of the twins anyway—says, disappointment curling his words.

His brother joins, bobbing his head in agreement. "I've never seen dark circles that aggressive."

"Maybe on Aunt Brenda."

"Nah, her eyes had bags, but they weren't dark."

"What about Mr. Chapman? Remember our seventh-grade social studies teacher?"

"Oh yeah, definitely. Dude, you look like Mr. Chapman."

I stopped listening to the twins' asinine back and forth almost as soon as they opened their mouths. There's no way I'm willing to waste whatever limited pep I have left trying to follow their train of thought.

Instead, I cut in.

"Stop. Just stop. The relay starts in twenty. Make sure you're ready." The snarly tone pops out of its own accord, and I feel bad as they shrink a little under the vicious state of my voice. I forego an apology (it'll take too much energy) and toss my empty cup into the green bin before making my way toward the tree line.

The obstacle course looms large and splintery in a long rectangular clearing. Surrounded by pine trees and brush, the space stays cooler than the main lawn, which is clear-cut and open to the punishing August sun. The set of matching structures is old, probably as old as the camp itself, and in serious need of an update. If I owned the camp, this would be the next thing to renovate. Not only because I love playing capture the flag, it's also a lawsuit waiting to happen. But that won't deter me from going headlong into the competition. There's too much at stake for me to tread lightly on this round.

Besides, I'm pretty sure I could guilt Leilani into still going out with me if I lost, as long as I also broke a leg or the equivalent. But I'd rather not find out.

The rich smell of warm sap and dirt centers me as I walk the length of the obstacles. Breathing deeply, I take pleasure in the beams of sunlight streaming between branches. Each beam feels considerably warmer than the shadows between. The hot and cool, hot and cool reminds me of the competition I share with Leilani.

When I'm near her, the proximity has me punch drunk. Heat coils inside of me like a fiery boa constricting my lungs. I feel flush all over. Like when she caught me in the shower yesterday. No amount of sputtering lukewarm water could cool me down. Not with her eyes on me the way they were.

Fuck. I wanted to slip my hand around the back of her neck, pull her toward me and finally get a chance to taste her. The image of her sinking into the delight right along with me tickles my senses. I can smell her now. That citrusy icing scent that makes me think of a creamsicle. I bet the rest of her is just as sweet.

"Is this a new thing for you or have you always walked around camp popping boners and I've just never noticed?"

The question should have stopped me cold, but Leilani's husky chuckle has the heat returning full force. Still, I check in with myself and realize I do, in fact, have a semi. While I try to get it under control, I'm not embarrassed. Not with the memory of her lusty stare seared into my mind.

"Is it a new thing for you to focus on my dick or have you always creeped around checking campers for wood?" I fire back with an equally raspy reply.

"Trust me, Pratt," she says, and strolls forward, crosses her arms, and leans casually against the climbing wall frame. "The thought of your dick never crossed my mind until I caught you with a fist full yesterday."

"And now it's all you can think about."

Her cheeks pinken and I know it's true. She's been thinking about me naked. She releases one arm and fiddles with the frayed strings hanging off her little denim cutoffs. I watch, wishing my fingers were playing along the edge of the fabric instead. Then I scan down her long, tan legs to her trim ankles. A flash of wrapping a hand around each one skims through my mind and I realize my efforts to quell my hard-on are hopeless. Not while she stands there.

Looking positively fuckable.

Her low chuckle makes me shiver.

"I'm not helping things. Am I?" she asks innocently, taking a step closer.

"No," I croak.

"Making things harder?" She's even closer, and I realize the scent I'd been imagining earlier came right from the source. Sweet and heady and so close.

"Very much so." I swallow hard. She watches my throat bob and bites her lip.

She's within reach now. I could easily settle a hand on the back of her neck or grab her hips and pull her to me.

I won't, though.

Not unless she shows me she wants it.

But she doesn't stop in front of me. Instead, she slowly glides past, stopping only to whisper a single word in my ear.

"Good."

I shudder as her breath tickles the sensitive spot along my neck. By this point, I realize my erection is in the raging category and that she's accomplished exactly what she set out to do.

"Hey, Walker," I call to her. She lingers at the edge of the clearing, waiting to hear whatever it is I'm going to say. "You're going down."

"Only if you win that date." She shrugs and moseys off.

God, I'm in trouble.

Chapter Twenty

Leilani

I should feel bad, but I don't.

All's fair, blah, blah, as they say.

While what Hudson and I have going on is war and most definitely *not* love, it satisfies one of the categories. And I know one thing for certain . . .

Hudson Pratt will not win the obstacle course event.

"Should we go over the plan again?" Albert asks while stretching out his hamstrings. Dude's shorts are so short that I'm concerned his nuts will dangle out the bottom and get caught while cresting the climbing wall.

"What part aren't you clear on?" I ask. Because all our strategy consists of is having Kendrick stand by the A-framed wall to help stragglers up and over until it's his turn to run the course. We discussed ad nauseam what order we should go in. Frankly, the only thing I care about is going last. Something about crossing the finish line for the victory and seeing Hudson's face while he loses is too good to miss.

"Nothing," Albert concedes. "Guess I'm just a little nervous."

I walk over to my teammate, place a hand on each shoulder, and lean close. He grins up at me, ready to receive the wisdom or whatever he thinks I'm about to impart. "The faster you go, the less energy you'll have for nerves."

His face falls a little when he realizes that's all he's going to get in the way of a pep talk. I pat his shoulders and turn back to the group. Everyone seems pretty pumped for today's challenge, and I'm right there with them. The obstacle course is the event that I tend to dominate. Last year, our team may not have won the trophy, but we still broke the camp record for fastest obstacle completion in all of camp history.

Hudson and the rest of the Tidal Waves don't stand a chance.

Which, for some reason, imbues me with a brief sense of disappointment.

Thankfully, Counselor Clark's whistle bleats into the clearing, and the sensation quickly evaporates. As the shrill sound bounces off trees and splintery structures alike, the rush of excitement returns.

"There are seven flags at the platforms on the opposite side of each course," the young counselor begins, his voice breaking as he aims to project the rules. "Each team will send someone through the course one at a time to retrieve a single flag. Once the flag is brought back, the racer must Velcro it to a provided dowel and stand it up in one of the available slots. The next racer cannot start their turn until the previous racer erects their own flag. Teammates are allowed to help each other on the obstacles but cannot take over the retrieval or erecting of the flags. The first team to collect and hoist all seven flags will be named the winner of this round."

Campers surround the clearing; some stand so close to the obstacles that they'd surely be smushed if one of us were to fall off. A few of them hold our mysteriously complete *Hudson Sucks* sign at chest level. Matching streaks of paint decorate their faces. The excitement is palpable and I have a moment of gratitude for being able to participate in camp each year. But that peaceful sensation is wiped away as guilt for potentially banning Hudson from the same joy takes hold. But I can't linger on it for long because Clark is shrieking for us to get into position.

We huddle up, place our hands in a circle, and shout a bawdy "Hudson Sucks" before lining up to start.

I glance over at my nemesis and see that he is at the back of his line too.

He arches a brow at me. His message is clear.

Game on.

I almost feel bad for him. Like perhaps I shouldn't have made the wager and given him false hope that he'd have a chance to take me out after this week. And his exile from camp? Something tells me the poor guy will miss our yearly competition.

But he's an adult. It's not on me to dictate what he agrees to put on the line.

"Everyone ready," Clark bellows.

Both teams hoot and holler. The crowd joins in. Electricity hums through the clearing.

One long whistle pierces the elevated din.

The start is a blur of action. Between Albert taking off, Kendrick speeding to the wall to take his position, and the cheering campers watching on the sidelines, the energy is insane. My body goes through the motions of encouraging my teammates, but my attention is divided. From the corner of my eye I catch the movements of my competitors. Jemma starts the relay; it's a smart move. She's smoking Albert, who pays more attention to preventing splinters in his bare, greased legs than keeping up with the little dynamo's lightning speed. By the time he reaches the wall and steps a foot into Kendrick's sizeable palms to be hoisted up to the top, she's already cresting the platform at the opposite end.

Dammit.

The strategy to order my teammates from slowest to fastest may have been a bad choice. The pressure for the last of us to make up the time will be substantial.

On instinct, I glance over at Hudson and find his eyes on me. That smirk, that fucking smirk, elicits a rage response that heats my neck and shoulders. It's clear he sees the discrepancy between our lead racers and feels great about it. With everything I have, I aim a look his way that says *don't start celebrating yet, asshole.*

He waggles his brows back at me as if to say *my chances look pretty good, Walker.*

To which I roll my eyes with a clear *whatever.*

Wait. When the hell did we develop the ability to have a conversation without talking? The idea that we know each other well enough to have a whole discussion with mere looks is unsettling.

Unnerving.

Screw that.

So, to wash away the unwelcome vibes produced by the silent conversation, I hold up my middle finger. No connection—deep or otherwise—needed to understand that gem.

He chuckles and turns back to his team, right as Jemma erects the first flag and tags one of the twins to start his turn.

Out on the obstacle course, Albert pops up over the wall facing us and labors to pull himself over. He's panting, sweaty, and red-faced. I'm suddenly overwhelmed with guilt because I find I'm worried we'll be disqualified if he passes out and not worried about his safety if he *does* pass out.

Competition does this to me. Call it a byproduct of having so many siblings who succeed at everything they do. Each one either went into professional sports or obtained some doctorate or another. Two doctorates in my youngest brother Doug's case. I don't even get the added benefit of being the only girl. Instead, I sit kind of in the middle of four brothers and a sister, all high achievers. For the longest time, I leaned into the sub-par middle-ish child schtick. Eventually, though, I decided the mediocre label I'd worn wasn't enough for me and I've been spending every ounce of energy trying to live up to my siblings' successes since.

And lemme tell you . . . it's no walk in the park.

But here at camp, I stand out. Because of my boisterous

rivalry with Hudson, I'm well-known among the regular campers and staff. The persona I project sets me squarely in a category of winners. Here, I'm successful. And I fucking eat it up every year.

Albert's huffing and wheezing break me out of my thoughts. His flag is securely in place. After tagging the next person in line, he sinks to a squat, sweat dripping down his face while he gasps for air like he finished a half-marathon rather than a summer camp obstacle course.

He looks up to me expectantly because, oh right, I'm the team captain.

"Good, um, hustle," I offer in my best little league coach voice. I briefly pat his shoulder, trying with all my might to hold back a cringe now that my hand is covered in his perspiration.

He smiles weakly and gets back to the work of sucking in air to replenish the oxygen in his poor, depleted body.

When my attention returns to the race, I'm pleased to find Linda has made up some time. The gap between Hudson Sucks and the Tidal Waves is no longer quite as dismal.

The next few teammates fly through the course, running on adrenaline and the energy drinks we all chugged while stretching. Kendrick helps the last person back over the wall before his turn and immediately returns to the platform to take his place.

The second-to-last Tidal Wave racer is already on the first obstacle as Kendrick joins me at the start.

"Think you can make up the difference?" I ask, my heart beating furiously in my chest.

He glances over his shoulder at me, a handsome grin playing out over his masculine features. A mist of sweat glistens at his salt and pepper temples. He huffs a little laugh, "Please."

I nod in approval, feeling a slight urge to give him a go-get-'em smack on the ass, but I hold back. For years there's been a slight hint that Kendrick's been interested in me and while I wish the feelings were mutual, they're not. I'd really hate to lead the guy on.

"You got this," I offer with a lame thumbs-up instead.

He winks at me right as another one of our teammates tags him to begin. The power behind his start is impressive. The man is built like a brick house, and I can't help but be in awe of his speed. He blows through each obstacle like he's leaping over a set of tinker toys my nephew cobbled together. He's quickly gaining on the other twin's progress, and by the time the opposing team's flag is grabbed, he's already surpassed his competitor.

Pride for having chosen a solid team (Albert notwithstanding) fills me with a lightness. As though I'm floating, watching the race from above rather than preparing to run my leg of it. But that cloud-like feeling is marred by something I can't quite pin down. Something heavy that pulls me back to my feet. Defining it is tricky, but all I can identify is that it's diminishing my high.

One look at Hudson is all it takes to see that the gloat from earlier has dissipated a bit. Worry lines rim his eyes and mouth. He wants this win badly. It's only then that I realize I might be the tiniest bit disappointed if I do win and miss out on our date.

Ridiculous.

Nothing has changed between us. Nothing that matters anyway. And I'm certainly not into Hudson. I'll admit I think he's hot, but his character squashes any notion that I'd possibly consider dating him.

"Get ready, Lei!" Kendrick's holler is fit for a warrior. Gruff and breathless. Like he just wailed on enemies at the frontlines in hand-to-hand combat. He's who I should be lusting over.

Not Hudson.

My teammate leaps onto the platform a solid obstacle ahead of Luthor and scrambles to Velcro his flag to a dowel. As soon as he's slid it into the assigned slot, he slaps my palm with his.

That tag seems to dispel all distractions and fills me with an excitable urgency because all I see is the balance beam ahead of me. I make quick work of it, scurrying one foot in front of the other to reach the other side. At the end, I leap down to the grass and haul over to the rings. These are a breeze and thanks to frequent trips to the playground near my oldest brother's house, I'm able to skip two at a time.

Sweat gathers and drips down from my hairline. I swipe it away with the back of my hand before it can reach my eyes and blind me. As I approach the wall, I grab the rope and start the incline. Kendrick had offered to help me here like he did with everybody else, but I knew I'd be more successful if I went at it alone. Running on pure excitement makes the wall a cinch.

Once I'm up and over, I dare to hazard a glance to see where Hudson is. It's a mistake because I see that he's gaining on me and is about to reach the wall on his side of the course.

Shit.

My focus returns to what's left. The army crawl, which is typically filled with mud but is blessedly dry. Not sure if someone forgot to wet it down or the change up was intentional. Either way, the lack of slop makes sliding on my belly beneath thin ropes that much easier.

One more obstacle before I hit the platform where the final flag hangs limp in the utter lack of breeze. The spinning log is by far the trickiest, but I've done it so many times that I know just how to move my body to react to the spin. In a blink, I'm hauling myself onto the platform and lunging for the final orange flag.

Which is the exact moment Hudson does the same on his side.

But instead of a flag the same as mine, I see that his is dark blue.

And lacy?

What the actual fuck?

My underwear.

That asshole is using the pair of panties I gave him last night as his fucking flag.

Rage faulters my step but only for the briefest of moments because it also refuels me. The ache in my legs vanishes, the air in my lungs is plentiful, and the sweat and dust coating my body and clothes feel more like war paint than byproducts of the obstacles.

I cram the flag down my shirt and into my sports bra so both hands are free, and leap off the platform to bolt back through. The log blinks by in a matter of quick leaps, I've never crawled through the dirt so fast in my life, and the climbing wall . . .? *Pfft*, what wall?

The other campers watch and shriek in overwhelming excitement. A blending of chants and shouts blur together and the only thing discernible in the mass of it is the syllables of my name. So many people are yelling it, waving their hands manically. There's no time to be touched by the encouragement right now. I'll be sure to thank everyone later this week when I accept the trophy at closing ceremonies.

But first, I need to finish this.

I press on, sprinting with the wild abandon of someone who has nothing on the line but sweet victory. As I blow through the rings and start the balance beam, I catch movement out of the corner of my eye. From what I can tell, Hudson's a few steps behind but gaining.

I race harder, despite the ache in my lungs. I'm sucking breath more frantically than ever before. I ignore the scream of my palms, scraped from the sharp gravel of the dirt pit and the burn of the rope that aided me up the wall.

So close.

Bracing myself on the edge of the platform, I leap up. All the while my team is shouting at me, but I can't make anything out. My focus is singular and I've almost achieved it. I grab for the final dowel while teetering on wobbly legs.

Wood palmed in one hand, I reach the other down my shirt to grab the flag. Once it's attached, it will all be over.

I will have won.

Hudson will have lost.

And we can forget this stupid date flight of fancy that he suddenly decided to throw at me. Forget the weird off-balance sensation I have when I think too hard about *us* in the outside world.

Because there is *no* us.

To prove it, all I have to do is—

Wait a minute . . .

I swipe my hand around in my bra, searching desperately for the little orange flag that will proclaim my success. But it's not there. I pull my neckline out and look for the bright triangle only to find boobs, shadows, and sweat.

Where the fuck did it go?

As I'm scanning the platform and surrounding obstacles, I finally see it. All the way across the course, lying limp and forgotten on the other platform. When I crammed it down my shirt I must have done so too hard and popped it right out the bottom.

By now, the other team is actively celebrating their win. Jumping and hollering and patting each other on the back.

I turn to my own team who looks at me with shock in their eyes. No one says anything, but I can feel their thoughts like shouts in my ear.

How could you drop the flag?

I flounder to think of something to say—to find some way to make it all better.

"Crap." Solid start, Leilani. "I'm sorry guys. I—I'm so sorry."

Kendrick throws his arm around me. "Don't worry about it, chick. We lost this one, but there's always tomorrow."

His comforting squeeze does little to erase how shitty I feel right now. And what's worse is that none of my teammates seem mad, only disappointed, which is somehow so much worse.

Chapter Twenty-One

Hudson

The spray from the shower isn't exactly satisfying, but watching the dust and grime swirl around and disappear down the drain certainly is. After the Tidal Waves won the obstacle course round of capture the flag earlier today, I thought my mood had reached its peak. But as I inch toward cleanliness, my spirits lift even higher.

My team was so happy and excited. Frankly, I didn't think we'd pull it off. Not with how much ground Kendrick and Leilani gained at the end. But she dropped the flag. No one saw that coming. Least of all me. She'd pushed so hard through her turn that you'd think she'd sprouted wings. The woman was determined to win, which leaves me wondering if she dropped the flag intentionally.

The notion is ridiculous. There's no way Leilani Walker

would ever throw a competition. Let alone one where having to go out with me was on the line.

Maybe deep down in her subconscious, *something* made her drop it.

I snort with laughter and crouch down so water can run over my face. The lukewarm trickle snaps me out of it. The flag drop was an accident, plain and simple.

I reach for the soap and start sudsing when the slap of flip-flops enters the men's shower. The sound bears a striking resemblance to when Leilani and her friend Mel walked in on me yesterday. The only difference is that there is only one set this time.

Arousal zings up my spine and I'm flooded with lust and memories from our earlier encounter. Has she returned for another session? Perhaps one with a bit more contact? Or *any* contact?

I debate whether calling out is wise or if it'd scare her off. She hasn't said anything yet and why would she if her goal is literally to shower and nothing else? Maybe the last thing she wants is for me to hit on her and remind her of the loss from this afternoon.

Following the obstacle race, someone started an impromptu party right there on the course. Two dudes carried out a large red bucket filled with ice and various canned beverages. Someone else flipped on a dusty old boom box that looked similar to the one I got on my tenth birthday. Right down to the Beastie Boys album I played on repeat until the CD got scratched beyond repair.

Everyone stuck around and whooped it up for a while.

Even Leilani's crew. Her teammates seemed to shake off the loss quickly while their fearless leader shot murderous looks at me the whole time. All I could do was grin, raise my panty flag at her, and wait for her to flip me the bird.

After a while, I bowed out in favor of cleaning up before dinner. Perhaps Walker has done the same.

The slap of her sandals inches closer and I continue to debate whether announcing my presence is a good plan. But then she pulls back the curtain right next to me, and I can't help myself.

"Back for another show?" I croon, my hard dick already in hand. I'm praying I'll get the chance to see some of her this time, but will happily settle for having her watch me again while I ease the tension.

My body jolts as a deep, manly chuckle bounces off the shower walls. I instantly soften.

"Sorry, bud. Clearly, I'm not who you hope I am."

"Kendrick?" I accidentally muse out loud.

"In the sweaty, about to be naked flesh," he replies, pulling his plastic curtain closed and turning on the weak shower.

"Fuck. Sorry." This time, the heat swimming through me is rooted in embarrassment.

"No problem, brother." He leaves it at that, but I feel the need to explain myself.

"I thought you were someone else." *Clearly.*

Next to me, Kendrick sighs as he steps into the spray. "And who might that be?"

I could tell him it was Leilani. For a moment I actually

consider it because I've seen the way this behemoth looks at her. With lust and longing. Fuck, it's the same way I look at her. So maybe if I tell him what went down with us, I could boot him out of her orbit. Stake a feeble claim. The desire to share flits away almost as quickly as it appears, replaced with a stronger desire to protect her privacy. So, I lie.

"Charles."

"Oh. *Really?*" Kendrick asks. "Wait, isn't he married?"

"No." This is quickly getting out of hand. "I'm mean yes, but—" Fuck, what do I mean? "It's an inside joke, is all. Goes way back to when we first met."

He chuckles heartily while squeezing what's probably shampoo into his hand. "Must be a good story. What happened?"

When did this guy become so chatty and inquisitive?

"You had to be there," I insist, hoping he drops it so we can change topics. Or stop talking altogether since we're, you know, showering next to each other. Why did he pick the stall next to mine? Isn't it like urinal rules? Space out unless there aren't any other options?

"Good game, by the way," he offers jovially.

So, we're still talking, then? Fine.

"Thanks, man. You too," I clip, hoping he'll get the hint and let me finish in peace.

"Bummer about Leilani dropping the flag. Really thought we had the win."

"Hmm," I hum noncommittally. I thought so too.

"Could have happened to any of us. I don't like how shitty she feels about it, though." He pauses a moment and I think that's the end of that until he clears his throat and starts again. "Don't rag on her about it."

It's a simple request, one I'd probably ignore—even while I detect the threat in his voice—if it weren't for the fact that I'm head over heels for her. But while the back and forth we sling can get petty, I wouldn't want to actually hurt her feelings.

It all makes me wonder if I should bow out of our bet. Let her off the hook so she can enjoy the remaining time here at camp rather than dread having to go out with me. The tricky part is that I'm really starting to think she and I could maybe be a good fit. I want to prove to her that the camp version of me isn't the same as real-life me.

All I need is a chance to show her.

"Nah, man. Don't worry about it," I assure Kendrick, still irked that he's the one looking out for her. "I'll lay off."

Chapter Twenty-Two

Leilani

This is a bad idea. Really, the worst idea in the world. I should turn around and head back into my cabin to wait for my turn in the shower. Instead, I close the door behind me and make my way down to the showers near the guys' cabins.

No matter how hard I convince myself that I'm going that way because I'm sweaty, gross, and impatient, the bitch in the back of my head mocks me. *You're just hoping to run into Hudson again,* she scoffs. *A naked Hudson. A soaking wet, naked Hudson.*

Earlier, when I left the post-race party, I moseyed past the showers and balked at the line winding out of the women's entrance. There's no way I'd get anywhere near a showerhead in the next two hours if I went that route. Really, my best bet would be to stay in my cabin and wait for the two ahead of me to take their turns.

But again, I'm sweaty, gross, and impatient.

So, I skulk to the men's shower in hopes that it's as empty as it was yesterday.

I try to convince myself that no one will be in there. Dudes shower so quickly that it's unlikely anyone will still be at it. What's most likely is that the women waiting in that long ass line got fed up and helped themselves to the other side of the building, which would be fine by me.

If not, I'd have the place to myself. Bonus.

And let's say Hudson *was* there. So what? Would it really be an issue? We could give each other space, shower in our respective stalls without incident. It's no big deal.

Then why am I low-key turned on by the prospect of him being there? Why does it work me up thinking I might see what he hides under those hoodies or that huge cock of his again? He's my nemesis. I loathe everything he stands for. Seeing him naked shouldn't be enough for me to abandon my principles.

And yet, here I go, slinking closer and closer to where I might be able to find him soaping himself up to wash away the grime from his win.

Ugh. The event was brutal.

I can't believe I fucked up as badly as I did. I've felt like shit since it went down, and not even a couple of beers were enough to take the sting off.

You know what?

I need this.

I need something to take my mind off the epic failure that was the race today. And maybe Hudson is just the man for the job.

Squaring my shoulders, I pick up the pace along the gravel path. Worst case scenario, I get quick access to a shower. Best case, I get that *plus* a show. Maybe I'll even join Hudson in his stall this time.

As I walk closer, I can hear water flowing from one of the showers. Clearly the women haven't happened upon the gold mine that is the bay of empty stalls, because the line still wraps around one corner. So, I check to see if the coast is clear and inch inside.

I'm careful not to let my presence be known, slip off my sandals to keep my feet quiet.

But then I stop dead because I hear a voice that doesn't belong to Hudson.

"Good game, by the way." My best guess is it's Kendrick.

"Thanks, man. You too." That's Hudson. Shit, he's in here but not alone, and while Kendrick's a dish, I'm not into the idea of making it some Eiffel Tower situation.

What I'm not above is eavesdropping a little. I am human after all.

"Bummer about Leilani dropping the flag. Really thought we had the win." Kendrick again.

The comment feels like a pile-on. Not from Kendrick, mind you, but from the universe screwing with me for listening in on a conversation not meant for my ears. But do I leave to shower elsewhere?

"Hmm," Hudson hums.

"Could have happened to any of us," Kendrick continues. "I don't like how shitty she feels about it, though. Don't
rag on her about it."

I smile a little, my heart a bit lighter knowing that my
teammate isn't upset with my screwup. Granted, to him, it's
probably only a game. Not something to be mad about.

Hudson speaks up.

"Nah, man. Don't worry about it. I'll lay off."

One shower cuts off.

Now's the time to scurry out of here. If either of them
comes out of their stall and sees me lurking, I'll never be able
to live it down. They'd have license to mock me for summers
to come, which isn't something I want to grant either of
them. Plus, Hudson would know I came looking for him.

I make my way out of the building and hotfoot it back to
my cabin.

"Decided to wait for this shower?" Mel asks as I reenter
the stuffy room.

"Lines were too long on the girls' side, and too many
wieners on the guys' side." Which is not a total lie. The addi-
tion of Kendrick's was one too many for me.

She smiles warmly and gestures ahead of herself. "Wanna
go ahead of me?"

My sweet, kind, sacrificing Melody. Always putting
everyone else first.

"No thanks," I say. "I can wait."

Chapter Twenty-Three

Third Year of Camp: Leilani

"Don't you think you might be taking this a little too far?" Bianca grips my wrist to stop me as I head for the stage so Hank and Jolly can announce the winners of this year's capture the flag tournament.

I marvel at this because Bee is never the voice of reason. She once convinced me to sneak into the men's locker room during a swim meet and steal all their clothes. Don't worry, they were our opponents—I'd never do that to our team. Lemme tell you, watching twenty-five college guys with swimmer's bodies striding to their bus carrying empty duffel bags and wearing nothing but sneakers and Speedos was a sight to behold. Or there was a time she drove us down to Portland on a whim and entered us into an amateur pole dancing competition. We did not win, if you're curious. All we walked away with was glitter in every crevice and the lingering scent of strawberry body oil that took a week to wash away. The worst part was driving back early in the morning so I could make it to my eight a.m. econ exam.

You get my point, though.

Bianca is the one who talks people *into* things, not *out of* things.

Which is why her worried expression gives me pause.

"Maybe we didn't win," I say with a shrug and pull from her grasp. I hold up a blue gift bag that says *Congrats* on one side in sparkly text. "Then this'll be moot."

"You're ruthless," she chuckles as I weave my way through the crowd. Members of my team fall in line to follow me to the front.

Hudson and his team, the Falconers, wait for me at the bottom of the steps.

"After you," he practically purrs. I take the lead and climb up the stage, even though I'm suspicious I'll end up with a kick me sign on my back. But Hudson waits for me and the rest of my Lord of the Flags teammates to stand on one side of the Beaumonts before he and the Falconers join us on the opposite side.

Hank steps forward with a beaming grin, his white, wiry hair fluttering in the breeze. He hooks a thumb under one of his suspenders and speaks into the microphone.

"These two gave it a mighty valiant effort this year. Best competition I've witnessed since the 2014 Super Bowl when the Seahawks destroyed the Broncos forty-three to eight." He pauses, chuckling to himself and shaking his head. "I exaggerate, of course. But you young people put on an entertaining spectacle nonetheless."

He studies Hudson, then me, and I can't help but notice the twinkle in his sapphire eyes.

"You know, when I opened Evergreen Adventure Camp in '69, this beauty"—he nods to his wife standing behind him—"walked in to apply. And even though we butted heads, I knew I'd be a fool not to hire her. Shortly after, I realized I'd be a fool not to marry her. So, I—"

He cuts off as Jolly settles a hand on his shoulder. Her smile is broad, and her eyes shine with so much affection that I feel a pinch in my chest. "Now's not the time for memory lane, dear."

"I suppose you're right, my love." He pats her hand and turns back to the remaining campers, who are waiting patiently for the capture the flag results.

Witnessing the Beaumonts' affection makes me homesick. My folks are adorably similar. Always looking out for one another and speaking kindly to each other. After nearly forty-five years of marriage and six kids later, they are just as smitten as Hank and Jolly appear to be.

It makes me wonder if I'll ever find my person. Lately, it's felt like that would only happen if I lowered my standards, and since that's not going to happen . . .

Astrid walks over and hands Hank a little envelope.

My wistfulness fades, replaced by an antsy feeling to find out who won as he tears the flap open and pulls out a pink index card.

"This year's winners are the Lord of the Flags!" he shouts into the microphone.

My team and I jump around in celebration, high-fiving and hollering into the warm summer air. I knew we'd win. Losing to Hudson last year was a slip-up, a fluke. I'd been so shocked by his unanticipated return to camp that it had thrown me off. But I knew what to expect this time around. Knew to be ready.

My shoulders instantly relax. All feels right in the world as Jolly brings us the old, beat-up trophy. My team hops and cheers some more as I mosey over to a red-faced Hudson. His fingers shake slightly as he runs them through his floppy brown waves and struggles to swallow.

It's almost like he's trying to find the words to say goodbye.

But not to me . . .

"Ready?" I ask sweetly, swinging the gift bag on one finger.

His brows slam together. Worried, hazel eyes dart from my face to the bag and back like he's searching for the punch line to a horrible joke. "You're not actually going to, are you?"

I glance up at the clear sky and tap my lips like I'm considering letting him off the hook. But the momentary hope melts off his face as I shrug and say, "You can do it. If it'll make you feel better."

"Just fucking get it over with," he snarls and turns away from me.

"Hey, Astrid. Can I snag that chair for a minute?" I call

to my favorite counselor, who is standing at the back of the stage wringing her hands together.

This year, Hudson and I made a big show of what we each put on the line. Everyone— campers, counselors, kitchen staff, the Beaumonts, even the groundskeepers— knows the stakes, which is probably why everyone stuck around. Normally, at least half of the guests have left by now, and besides counselors, the rest of the staff rarely attend closing ceremonies.

Astrid doesn't say anything but brings the folding stool over and hands it to Hudson, who is wearing a mask of remorse. He accepts it, slams it down on the wood planks of the deck, and sits, all while refusing to look at me.

I reach into the gift bag. The crowd titters and murmurs as I pull out cordless hair clippers.

"Let's see, how do these things work?" I feign ignorance. Hudson physically startles when I flip the trimmer on and it buzzes loudly. I snap the off switch and chuckle. "Seems easy enough."

"Leilani," Hudson growls. He's breathing heavily, clearly stressed about losing all that thick, luscious hair.

"Ok, ok. Just trying to figure out the best plan of attack." I step forward. Bag in one hand, clippers in the other. To get under his skin, I flip them on and off a few times. I swear the torment is the sweetest part of doling out his punishment.

"*Leilani.*" His slow enunciation of the syllables in my name is full of warning. And a shiver runs down my back.

"You're no fun."

I buzz the clippers a couple more times and start riffling

through the bag for the right hair guard attachment. Hudson's knee bounces rapidly. He's impatient.

But before I can attach the guard to the blade, he turns and snatches the trimmer from my hands and swipes it down the center of his scalp. My jaw hangs open, my now-empty hand hangs frozen in the air.

Aside from the whirring buzz and creaking of the stool Hudson is sitting on, everyone is silent. We watch as clumps of hair fall all around him, making a chocolatey halo around the bottom of his stool. After what seems like forever, he turns to me.

For the most part, his head is coated with short, uneven stubble aside from a few straggling hairs he missed in his blind sweeps. He steps close. Looms over me.

"Happy?"

I don't respond at first. But as I hold up the bright pink guard that would have left him with an inch of hair to work with, I croak out a few words. "I was gonna use an eight."

His eyes boomerang from me to the bit of plastic in my hand. Understanding and regret for being so hasty dawn on his face. There's much less rage than a moment ago.

"I guess beanie season's starting early this year," he says dryly, like he was trying to make a joke but couldn't manage the necessary intonation. He drops the clippers to the deck, pulls the hood of his sweatshirt up, steps around me, and strides toward the parking lot.

Chapter Twenty-Four

Friday Morning: Leilani

"A little food will do you some good," Melody soothes as though I'm her son after he lost a soccer match.

My growling stomach emphatically agrees, drawing teasing looks from other campers who are also in line for breakfast. The waft of yeast and cinnamon speaks to my soul, waging war against the mood-altering hunger pushing me further down in the dumps. Friday is always the big fancy breakfast, flush with cinnamon rolls, French toast, and all the morning meats. It's a massive leap up from the oatmeal and rehydrated scrambled eggs we're served the rest of the week. Normally, the breakfast smorgasbord is my absolute favorite, but dwelling on yesterday's screw up dims my excitement.

"You're hangry, I get it," my friend says, misinterpreting my silence for anger. That emotion left me almost instantly once the Tidal Waves were announced victorious. What quickly replaced it was embarrassment, shame, and a little something I can't quite identify. For a moment, I thought it might be hope, but I quickly washed the notion away with a cold can of Rainier and enough water to drown an elephant.

Melody doesn't say anything further, presumably opting to let me be until I've shoveled a few forkfuls of sugary goodness into my mouth.

The line inches forward, and soon it's our turn at the buffet setup. I pile my plate high with a massive iced roll, two of every meat varietal, and—since I'm not a complete heathen—a big scoop of fruit salad. No, my eyes are not too big for my stomach; I intend to polish off every bite.

Soon, we're sitting at one of the many cafeteria-style tables that fill the mess hall. Mel sits across from me, opens her napkin to place across her lap, and inhales an appreciative sniff of breakfast. Such pomp and circumstance are in direct opposition to the way I commence shoveling. The food is delicious and I quickly find my mood improving, realizing that perhaps low blood sugar *was* partially to blame for my grouchiness. Half done, I come up for air and wipe a fistful of napkins over my face. I've made such a mess that I have to fold them in on themselves and go in for another swipe.

Mel watches me with the sweetest, loving smile. One I'm helpless not to return.

"Better?" she asks me.

"God, yes."

She nods once and only then digs into her meal.

"Sorry for being grouchy," I offer sheepishly before returning to my plate.

She taps a napkin to her lips and shakes her head. "I've known you for a long time, Leilani Walker. No need to be weird about it. I'm glad you're feeling better."

I smile again, feeling immensely grateful to call this woman my friend.

"Leilani!" From the cafeteria door, Bianca bellows my name so loudly that most of the crowd stops and turns to see what the problem is. She scurries frantically around the tables trying to track me down. "Leilani, will you make yourself known, goddammit?"

Mel holds up her napkin and waves it while I ignore the commotion and keep chipping away at my breakfast.

Bianca spots us and speeds over.

"Have I got the scoop for you," she whispers loudly and shoves my hip with hers to sit on the end of my bench. I begrudgingly oblige and shift so she has room. She clocks our plates and dons a confused expression. "Why are they doing the big breakfast on a Thursday?"

Mel's fork stops halfway to her mouth. "It's Friday morning," she corrects.

Bianca turns to me. "Really?"

I nod, swirling a pork sausage in syrup then biting off half of it.

"Well, I'll be." She reaches over to snag what's left of my cinnamon roll. I slap the back of her hand, but she takes it anyway.

Mel and I look at her expectantly. Mostly, I glower at her as she sinks her teeth into my sweet treat.

"Where's the fire?" Mel finally inquires. She sneaks her

roll onto my plate. I smile and return it because I'm not taking the tiny sliver she took for herself.

Bianca squints in confusion until her memory kicks back in. "Oh, right." She tosses her half-chewed pastry onto the table and dusts crumbs from her fingers. "Eddie was eating me out in the pump house on the outskirts of camp this morning and I saw something interesting."

Mel snickers.

"Not great at the oral exam, huh?" I ask teasingly.

"Why would you ask that?" Bianca asks.

"Because you had the presence of mind to notice other things."

She grins mischievously. "Someone has to be the lookout, and since his vision was obscured . . ."

"Fine," I say, trying to move it along. "What did you spy with your little eye?"

"Something orange," Bianca answers while pulling a strip of bacon from my dwindling plate.

"Bee. Quit with the bullshit and tell us what up," I growl as she wiggles the floppy meat around before popping it into her mouth.

"It was a flag for tonight's game. My guess is they started putting them out early, which seems silly since there's a chance *someone*"—she points to herself—"might find them."

Interesting.

I never would have thought to look out there. Typically, the flags are hung up in trees or taped under picnic tables, but the pump house is so far out there. I thought it was off limits. They must have extended the boundaries of the game this year.

Suddenly, something about her telling me where to find a flag feels wrong. Which makes sense because it's cheating. Even though she offered the information rather than me asking for it. I refuse to win by ill-gotten means.

"Thanks for the hot tip," I say, returning to my meal. "But I won't be going after that one."

"What? That's lame. Why not?"

"It's cheating," Melody cuts in before I can say the same thing. "Leilani wants to win fair and square."

Bianca looks to me, silently asking if what our friend says is the truth.

"Sorry," I say with a shrug.

"Suit yourself," Bianca says as she rises from the table. "Later, ladies."

"Wait." I grab her by the wrist to stop her from leaving. "Is Eddie going to tell Hudson?"

I may not want to win by cheating, but I have to know if Hudson would if the roles were reversed.

Bianca shakes her head, and I notice a hickey the size of a silver dollar on her neck. "Nope. You're in the clear."

"How can you be sure?" I ask. Why I'm desperate to know what Hudson knows makes no sense, but I push anyway.

"Because," our friend says, grinning. She snatches the cinnamon roll chunk she gnawed on from the table again and pulls from my grasp. "I had his head squeezed so tightly between my legs that there's no way he saw anything but stars."

Chapter Twenty-Five

Hudson

"Is everyone clear on their roles?" I ask, scanning my teammates one at a time.

My question is met with enthusiastic nods and one snarling blonde who cracks every single one of her knuckles. Against the variety of athletic and casual wear everyone is dressed in, Jemma looks like she's prepared to storm an enemy camp in the jungle. Brown, black, and green paint cover not only her face but all exposed skin. The rest of her is cloaked in clingy black fabric. The black beanie caps off the ensemble, likely to hide the golden lightness of her hair. The level of seriousness that she takes when playing capture the flag is impressive. So much so that I'm considering passing the team captain torch to her after this year.

I've been giving it a lot of thought, and I think that even if we win, this might still be my last stay at Camp Clandestine. I love coming here. The escape from reality is great, but now that I've made my intentions regarding Leilani clear, returning might be tricky if my affections remain unrequited.

If my team wins today, she's guaranteed to go out with me back home. At that point I'll pull out all the stops and do my damnedest to show her who I really am. Show her what she means to me, what we could mean to each other.

But if we lose, I won't get a chance to show her. Worse than that would be if I win, we do go out, but she decides she still loathes me. Rubbing salt in the wound every year following the rejection doesn't sound like the fun, carefree experience I've come to love.

A sudden wave of nostalgia surprises me as I consider this will likely be my very last CTF event.

"We're clear," Luthor and Lex say in unison as though they planned it out ahead of time.

"Perfect." I nod. "Be sure to hydrate. Game starts in fifteen."

High fives are exchanged, and we all disband for whatever preparations we need to do prior to the whistle.

Following my own advice, I step in line to fill my water bottle.

"At least you didn't cut this time." The silky lilt of her voice wraps me in longing. I can't help the smile that forms on my lips.

I turn to face Leilani, who stands directly behind me, Nalgene dangling from her fingertips. "I'm on the straight and narrow these days."

"Must be a challenge for you." Her brow quirks. She

scans me from head to toe before popping her gaze back to my face. The little flush that colors her cheeks sends a surge through me. I'd bet my car that she's imagining me naked—with absolute clarity—because what we shared was no fleeting glimpse.

The effort I employ to keep my eyes on hers is award-worthy. Though it still doesn't keep me from imagining what it would have been like if the shower roles had been reversed at some point. "I manage."

"This week flew by," she idly comments.

"Small talk? Really? Frankly, I'm disappointed in you, Walker." When she pulls back in surprise, I continue. "Where are the insults? The trash talk?"

"Maybe I'm trying to throw you off by being pleasant."

"That would be a first," I say cheekily.

Her eyeroll is so loud that it makes a laugh burst out of me.

"Fine, have it your way. We're going to destroy you."

"Good girl, that's more like it," I say huskily.

"How many times do we have to go over it, Pratt? Praise is not my kink." She crosses her arms across her chest and I'm helpless to resist a glance at the resulting cleavage. She scoffs while I ogle.

It's my turn to throw her off. I step in close so she has to tilt her chin up to look at me. "We'll go over it as many times as it takes for you to actually *tell* me what your kink is."

She raises slowly on her tip-toes, lips an inch away from mine. God she smells fucking amazing. All citrusy and sweet like some kind of summer treat ready to be devoured. Her hand curls around one of the strings on my hoodie, twiddling it around her fingers so they're good and wrapped in it.

"Get comfy in purgatory, then. Because I won't give that information up easily."

Despite the looming nightfall, the heat from the day lingers. It hangs stagnantly in the air like an invisible shroud, refusing to be lifted. But when she steps away, breaks the almost-contact between our bodies, an immensely disappointing chill sweeps through me. Her strides are smooth as she glides around me in line and steps up to the watercooler. Naturally, I turn and watch as she's bent over, filling her bottle to the rim and then some, so a bit trickles out the top and into the sunburned grass below it.

She giggles and stands upright. Caps her Nalgene and walks away without a word or backward glance.

Shaking my head, I place my bottle under the spigot. But the trickle of water that quickly dies elicits a curse from me. I glance at Leilani's retreating form only to be rewarded by her blowing me a kiss. It's meant to be mocking, but I happily accept it even as I lug the awkward orange cooler into the kitchen for a refill.

Chapter Twenty-Six

Leilani

Excitement and tension hum through the crowd as both teams gather together at the starting point in the middle of the field. Large floodlights illuminate the immediate area, leaving the perimeter of the field in what feels like utter darkness. Once we enter the woods our eyes will adjust. It's a full moon, and with a clear sky and lights in various parts of the campgrounds, seeing won't be that tricky. But the wash of false light where our teams and other observing campers stand gives the vibe that the earth drops off once you pass into the shadows.

"Welcome to the final round of capture the flag," Counselor Clark shouts. This is the first time I've seen him without his massive hat and face half-covered in zinc sunblock. The kid's a cutie but looks even younger with a clean face and exposed floppy haircut. "The multi-flag capture will determine the winner of this year's games. Over the next two hours, the team that finds and collects the most flags will be declared the winner. For a flag to count, it must be dropped into your team's basket before the whistle sounds."

"How many flags are there?" I ask because it varies each year.

"Fifty-three," Clark states.

There are gasps and murmurs, and it makes me giggle. To an outside observer you'd think a dollar amount was attached to each flag collected instead of a banged-up trophy and bragging rights. Still, that's twice as many flags as prior years.

"Flags may be attached to or beneath other objects, so you may have to move things, but you won't have to break into anything to retrieve them. If you come to a door that's locked or something is nailed shut, I promise you, there is nothing in there." The counselor looks pointedly at Jemma, who infamously busted the hinges off a tool shed last year during the final round...with her bare hands.

I instantly think of the pump house and the flag Bianca found this morning. I'll avoid it because while I refuse to cheat and claim it, I also don't want to inadvertently lead a competitor to it.

"Are there any more questions?" Clark looks around at all of us. He's satisfied when everyone shakes their head. "Get into position."

The boisterous onlookers recommence their whoops and chants. A group of campers holds my team's sign, which is looking a little worse for wear at this point. Mel leads the group in a rousing chant of "Hudson Sucks! Hudson Sucks!" Bianca stands beside her with a forlorn Eddie looking on. I wonder if they had a lovers' spat since their rendezvous at the pump house.

Counselor Clark raises the whistle to his lips, bursts out three long peeps, and we're off. The Tidal Waves clump together, entering the tree line as a unit. We take a different tactic and scatter in all directions. With as many flags as there are, it seems the most logical to divide and conquer.

Less than five minutes into the shadows and I've already found two flags. The first hung from a branch in the middle of the trail (child's play) while the other was a bit trickier, rolled up and taped to the back of a trail marker. In games past, I would have collected as many as possible and waited until the last minute to bring them back to our basket. But after what happened at the obstacle course yesterday, I refuse to take any chances.

I scan the immediate area for any more flashes of orange before turning tail and hauling ass back to the well-lit field. I'm the first to add to our score, but a quick glance in the Tidal Waves' basket shows there is at least one runner bringing flags back. It's impossible to know how many they have in there without a closer inspection, but I can tell it's more than we have in our basket.

"Leilani!" The shout comes from Bianca, who waggles her brows and nods her head in the direction of the pump house once we make eye contact.

I swat my hand in her direction and mouth an exaggerated *No* before turning and sprinting back into the darkness.

I refuse to cheat. If I'm going to beat Hudson this year, it's going to be a legitimate victory.

Deep in the woods, there's a rustling in the bushes beside me. A startled gasp escapes my lips. Whatever it is, it's big, and for a moment I wonder if I've stumbled on a bear or deer or something, until a cautious chuckle eases my worries.

"It's only me." Kendrick's voice is marred by heavy breathing as he climbs out of the brush and strides toward me.

"Did you find one?" I ask with relief.

He holds up his fist, where orange flags dangle in a crumpled mass. "Three so far. There was one behind that big boulder. Managed a few scrapes from blackberry vines, but that's what I get for wearing shorts. What about you?"

"Two, but I already took them to our basket."

"Sweet. Wanna pair up? Look together for a bit?" His suggestion is innocent enough, but for whatever reason, I'm certain there's an implication behind it. Could be my hyper-awareness that has me twitchy. Kendrick's a dish, but ultimately I'm not interested in him. I'd much rather see where things go with—

I cut my thoughts off with a sharp, audible hiss.

"What is it?" Kendrick asks, rushing forward and placing a hand on my cheek. "Are you hurt?"

But I haven't checked in with what he's asked because I'm far too distracted with where my traitorous mind was going. I don't know why I have to continually remind myself that I'm not into Hudson. Am I curious what a date with him outside of camp would be like? Sure. I'll admit that. But it's all morbid curiosity. Like stumbling across old yearbooks in your high school library only to find out that your steps-away-from-retirement math teacher used to be a smoke show. Or finding out the stuffy HR manager in your office writes erotic Disney fanfic. You can't *not* be curious.

I know what to expect from the camp version of Hudson. Snark, sarcasm, shower masturbation, apparently, which is new...and surprisingly titillating. But for the most part, it's clear where we stand in relation to each other.

Camp rivals or enemies or nemeses or some version of that.

We aren't potential partners.

Kendrick brushes the hair off my temple and tucks it behind my ear. For such a large man he's surprisingly gentle. Though I assume because of his size he's learned to adapt.

"Leilani?" his query pulls me back to the present. Back to the woods here at camp where I have a mission.

"Oh sorry, yeah." I place my fingers on his hand and remove it from my jaw. "I'm fine. Thank you for checking in."

His thick arm drops to his side, then he stuffs both hands into his pockets. "Did you want to search together?"

He's sweet. Really, he is. But he's not who I want.

"I think we should stick to the plan. Divide and conquer."

Kendrick nods, a smile drifting along his lips but failing to reach his eyes. It's clear he's disappointed, but fortunately not butthurt about the rejection. Dude won't have any trouble in the dating pool. Part of me wonders if he was just looking for a camp hookup. Either way, it doesn't matter. "Sounds good. I'm heading that way"—he throws a thumb over his shoulder toward the starting line—"to turn my flags in."

"Good plan." I chuckle. "Wouldn't want to drop those along the way like a certain someone yesterday."

His smile is genuine this time. "We wouldn't want that."

A moment later, I'm standing alone among the evergreens. Moonlight shines through the branches, lighting splotches of path and brush. Crickets chirp and leaves rustle as a light breeze picks up from Heartbreak Lake. With it comes blessedly cool relief. A much-needed change from the lingering heat of the day.

Though I struggle to enjoy any of it because I'm too distracted wondering what the hell is wrong with me and when I started crushing on the absolutely wrong man.

Chapter Twenty-Seven

Hudson

My blood boils.

It boils even though I have no right to her. Leilani loathes me. Ok, maybe loathe is the wrong word; that's a little too harsh. But she sure doesn't like me and that should be enough to send me packing.

Especially as I watch her standing in the moonlight, spots of tan skin illuminated under the evening glow. Kendrick stands before her, tucking a stray hair behind her ear. She doesn't shy away from the contact. In fact, she appears enthralled by his touch. There's no competing with the guy either. He's way bigger than me. Nicer, too. If they haven't hooked up in the past, this is probably the moment the winds change in favor of the big guy. I wouldn't be surprised if I'm witnessing the story of "how we got together" that they'll tell at their wedding. Or to their children. Or even their grand—

Wait a minute.

I watch as Leilani slides his hand off her cheek and steps back. There's a lot of head shaking, shoulder shrugging, and —ohh, poor guy—the empathetic head tilt. She's turning him down gently. I can't help but feel bad for the dude, if only for a moment.

Very quickly, however, determination takes its place.

Kendrick lumbers away, leaving Leilani alone on the path to the pump house that I was walking along before I saw what looked like an intimate exchange and stopped dead. I'm not proud of scurrying off the trail to spy, but certain stakes are on the line.

I waffle between making myself known and waiting for her to leave before resuming my search, but my feet have other plans.

"Lose your way, little lady?" I say in my best predatory big bad wolf voice, prowling toward my target.

Leilani doesn't startle. Instead, she tilts her head back and peers up at the sky as though she's praying for strength.

"What's in the basket, red?" I double down. Even as it leaves my mouth, I'm cringing. Too late now, I guess. I stop a few feet away from her.

"I don't have a basket." She turns and faces me.

"Sure, I see that," I mumble.

"And I'm not a redhead or even wearing red."

"I was doing a bit."

"A lame one," she mocks, though I'm starting to notice a teasing tone in her voice.

"Fine. The joke was dumb. Happy?"

She shrugs, and I decide it's time to move on. So, I turn and continue down the path in my original direction.

And I'm beyond pleased when I hear her steps pick up behind me. I'd follow this woman anywhere, but her tailing me—even if her motives hinge on suspicion—ignites an inferno inside my chest. I'm a hopeless pile of dry kindling and her closeness is a shower of sparks.

"Where are you headed?" she asks, full of accusation.

"Why do you think it's any of your business, Walker?" Even as I snark back at her, a smile pulls at my lips.

"Doesn't hurt to ask," she responds with faux casualness.

"The pump house." I shouldn't be telling her this. We're on opposite teams. If I were smart, I'd shake her off my tail. Pull some bait-and-switch maneuver so I can sneak away and get a step closer to victory. I still want to win the tournament. I'm aching to take her out on a date. To force her to give me a chance in the real world. But I'm short-sighted, because I'd give anything for her to follow me anywhere for any silly reason...even if it's around the woods for the next couple of hours.

"Why the pump house?" The accusation is back.

"Because there might be a flag there," I say, even though it should be obvious.

"There's nothing in the pump house," her words come out in a frantic jumble.

Her statement stops me short. Unaware of Leilani's close proximity, I turn, and we collide. My arms wrap around her on instinct—really, they must have a mind of their own—as we lose balance and topple. My fingers dig into the soft skin at her waist. I pull her close, attempting to absorb her impact as my back slams onto the dirt path. The ungraceful landing knocks the wind from my lungs, but her sprawled form on top of me keeps the breath from returning. My thumping heart has taken precedence over all other functions in my body. Every inch of me is hyper aware of her thigh pressing against my dick. She squirms a little, like my grip on her either tickles or sends her into a similar state of arousal.

By the time she braces a palm on either side of me and pushes back, I've finally managed to pull in air tinted with the sweet smell of her. I inhale another hit while she studies me.

"You ok?" she asks, a ragged quality marring her words.

I lick my lips and manage a jerky nod. Her eyes dip, watching my mouth.

She's breathing heavily too, and it takes every single ounce of strength not to snarl my fingers deep into her hair and kiss her.

But the spell is broken when she finally rolls off me and gets to her feet. I scramble up beside her, brushing dirt and pine needles off my jeans.

"That was fun," I say, attempting to take the edge off.

Leilani adjusts her ponytail and blows out a breath. "Sure," she offers.

After a weird moment of silence, I resume heading toward the pump house.

"What do you know?" She falls into step beside me, and I'm infinitely pleased she hasn't abandoned her relentless pursuit.

"What do I know about what?" I ask.

"The pump house?"

If she's trying to lead me away from the little utility building at the back of the woods, she's failing miserably. Because the more she grills me about it, the more determined I am to go there. It's clear she knows something about it and thinks I do too. But it's a hunch I've had since Clark said something about locked doors. Maybe the door is unlocked and there's a flag inside. It's worth a shot.

"I'm checking for a flag. Like I mentioned a minute ago before you tackled me." I hazard a glance and can't help but chuckle at her scowl.

"So, Eddie told you." Does she sound deflated?

"I've barely seen Eddie this entire trip. He's been busy with Bianca—as usual."

"Oh, uh. All right,"

"But now I'm quite certain there's one in there." I pick up my pace, trying to stay a step ahead of her.

Her violent curse is cute. As are her quickening steps as she tries to surpass me. I pick up speed, shifting from a fast walk to a lazy jog, but she pushes faster and soon I'm at an all-out run. The ramshackle hut is within sight. We race toward it, side by side.

I reach for the knob but she lunges ahead of me and steps in my path. The sight of her trying to block the door with her whole body is both adorable and incredibly sexy. I think about all the ways I could make her move. Consider if I even want to make her move. The way she's splayed out—arms raised, holding onto the top of the doorframe—has me aching to touch the strip of exposed skin at her waist. Play with the sparkling gem that dangles from her belly button.

I step close and settle a hand on her hip. She hisses in a breath, though I can tell it has nothing to do with disgust. The contact startles her, but by the state of her pupils and rise of her chest I'm certain she shares my hunger.

I scooch forward even more, the fabric of my hoodie grazes that tan strip of her belly, and for the first time ever I'm wishing I weren't wearing it.

"What are you doing?" she asks me. Her words are quiet, but the husky quality drags seductively against my skin.

"What do you think?" My breath shifts the escaped strands of hair that hang around her face and I momentarily thank past Hudson for brushing his teeth before the evening's event.

Leilani's eyes droop to half-mast. "Trying to make me move?"

"Not exactly, Walker." Quiet laughter rumbles deep in my chest. "I'm trying to make you squirm."

Chapter Twenty-Eight

Fourth Year of Camp: Hudson

I learned two very important things last year.

First, confidence won't always get you the win.

Second, it takes just about twelve months to grow six inches of hair. And since I started with a practically bald head last August, I'm grateful to be heading back to camp with the evidence of the previous year's loss completely erased.

Some of my naïve cockiness has faded over the last year too. As a result, there's no way I'll wager anything semi-permanent again, regardless of how confident I am going into the competition. Fool me once, ya know?

I'm pretty sure Leilani felt a little bad about how things went down at the fateful closing ceremonies. She must have found out where I worked from Charles because a couple of beanies showed up at my office addressed to The Douchebag from Camp AKA Hudson Pratt. Despite her snark, I could sense the underlying tone of apology in her gesture. I wore the hell out of those knit hats. Even after I had a shorter style I could live with, I peppered them into my outdoor wardrobe rotation. They reminded me of camp and the all-consuming competition of our tournaments.

Eventually, wearing them began summoning thoughts of her.

Besides, a beanie pairs well with a hoodie, in my humble opinion.

"You can't be serious," Leilani grumbles as she scans the words I labored over.

Perhaps labored is a bit dramatic. I scribbled them down last night while Charles and I watched from the deck as campers raved at the annual foam party.

"As a heart attack," I assure her.

We went a bit gentle with our wagers this year. If her team had won, I'd be donating fifty bucks per month for the rest of my working life to the teen center she runs in Tacoma. That amount wouldn't break the bank or anything, but I would have had to donate with a check under the pseudonym Bratty Pratty, which I wouldn't have loved so much.

"Fine." Leilani clears her throat and begins mumbling the poem I wrote for her performance.

"Wait. Stop," I say, stepping over to her.

"What?" she snaps, crumpling the paper in a fist before plunking it onto her popped hip.

I drink in the curve of her denim shorts, the same cut-offs

that seem to make more cameos in my fantasies than I care to admit.

"Say it with your whole chest," I teasingly scold. "And to me. Remember, you're reciting it to me."

Leilani rolls her eyes so hard I'm afraid they'll get lost in her skull, but she straightens out the smashed paper to continue. Before she can start, I touch the bottom of her elbow to encourage her to raise the microphone she's holding closer to her mouth.

"Like you mean it or I'll make you say it again and again until you do it correctly." I drop my hand away and take a few steps back.

Her jaw clenches with so much irritation that it makes her shiver a little. But as she closes her eyes and takes a few breaths, her rage calms—or maybe she's a great actress.

"*Why I love Hudson Pratt*," she says, and directs a scowl at me. So, naturally I helpfully remind her to enjoy herself. I chuckle at her grimace and accept it because that's the closest I'll get to a smile.

I'm ravenous to hear these words fall out of her plump lips. I'm so intently zeroed in on them that I almost miss the physical shift of her body.

Almost.

Suddenly, Leilani seems to morph in front of me. She lowers her eyelids in a sexy little flutter and inhales a deep breath, her tits rising intentionally, seductively.

"Hudson," her voice is a breathy moan, and my throat instantly goes dry. "You're a god among men."

She takes a step toward me, only it's more of a prowl than a walk.

"Anyone here would say you're a ten."

Why do I feel more like prey right now than someone who won a tournament and is collecting on a bet?

"You're so hot it's sick." She adds a hint of a whine, a little whimper, and it bears a striking resemblance to a few fantasies I've had of her in those very shorts while I've been away from camp.

"Bet you have a huge dick." She licks those pillowy lips before catching the lower one between her perfect white teeth. She's so close to me now. A jolt of lust zips to my cock and suddenly, I'm not feeling so confident in my wager decisions.

"I'm so happy," she continues, pressing her chest against mine. I release an unconscious groan, something guttural that completely gives away my response to her. "You spanked me again."

Her face is tilted up to me, the microphone and a breath arc the only things separating our mouths. This close I can see gold flecks in the depths of her brown eyes, even as her pupils dilate.

Oh, ho. Maybe I'm not the only one affected by her little poetry reading.

But before I can get ahold of myself or remember that we're in front of a couple hundred campers, she turns away from me and bows to roaring applause.

She's laughing, they all loved it, and I'm left standing on stage with a semi like this is some teenage nightmare come true. I casually slip my fists into the pockets of my hoodie and position it in a way that hides my predicament.

I've been bested by my nemesis, Leilani Walker.

"Satisfied?" she purrs in my direction.

That's not exactly the way I'd put it.

Chapter Twenty-Nine

Present Day, Friday Night: Leilani

I'm split in two. Warring versions of myself that want opposite things.

The sane part of me is blocking Hudson from entering the pump house. I brace myself against the doorframe in an effort to conceal what I know is in there.

The other part of me, the part that's a slave to the lust radiating off this man standing so close, is aching.

Aching for his touch.

Aching for him to slide his hands higher—or lower for that matter.

Aching to know what it feels like to have Hudson press his lips to mine and press his tongue deep into my mouth.

The minty sweetness of his breath leads to my undoing, a place where logic has no claim. And before I know it, I reach down, palm the weathered doorknob behind me and turn. It's loud. The rusty metal hinges creak obscenely as though boldly declaring my intent.

Hudson's choked groan mingles with the drag of the ancient wood, filling my senses with a rush of anticipation. He steps forward, guiding me back into the dark little building. I'm helpless to follow his lead. Not that I want to resist it. Something is breaking inside of me. A fight I no longer want to define myself by.

His lips hover above mine even as his fingers inch beneath my shirt.

Sure enough he has me squirming. I wait for him to finally fucking kiss me, but he doesn't. He holds the distance, that infinitesimal space where electricity seems to spark like static between us. Why isn't he kissing me? Why hasn't he claimed my mouth like we both desperately want?

A flash of irritation sizzles up my spine until understanding dawns.

He needs to *know* I want it.

That I want *him*.

He's refusing to close the gap on his own, demanding that I do my part and submit to the seedy attraction that's been brewing for four angsty years.

Four years is long enough.

I press up, offering my lips in a delicate sweep and that broken groan of his destroys me. My fingers slip into his hair, fisting the soft waves that flop over his brow in a perpetually sexy bedhead.

As he sucks my bottom lip between his and nibbles, I quickly realize Hudson isn't just kissing.

He's tasting me.

Savoring.

My knees weaken, but I don't fall. One large hand palms my ass, squeezing and supporting while the other runs up my back and beneath my sports bra.

Once we've cleared the door, he back kicks it shut. We plunge into near darkness, shutting out the slices of moonlight that lit our way to this place. I welcome it as it enhances my other senses. The taste of his toothpaste. The drag of his teeth and tongue along my jaw as he trails his way to the sensitive spot behind my ear. The press of his fingertips making divots in my flesh.

My back hits the wall. He cups the back of my thighs to coax me into wrapping my legs around his waist. I link my ankles behind him and am rewarded instantly with him pressing against my sex. A needy whimper fills the stale air of the pump house, bounces off the walls, and mingles with the rustle of our clothing and Hudson's shoes against the floorboards.

"Leilani Walker." He says my name like it's a cherished secret. An oath into the universe, thanking it for the gift he's receiving. His words hang there, playing over and over in my ear, and I almost wonder if he's chanting them or if his silky voice ricochets in my brain.

My eyes have adjusted to the dim, and I can see more details of our surroundings. Large barrel-type tanks jut from pipes coming up from the floorboards. Some kind of box, perhaps a control panel or breaker box, hangs on the wall beside them. The large components take up the bulk of the room. A little stool sits in the corner, presumably used for maintenance purposes. We're squeezed tightly into a space meant for one, but it's not uncomfortable.

He seems to notice my wandering attention and rolls into me to regain it. It's good but not enough. I want more. Need more. All of him.

I release fistfuls of his hair and grasp the bottom of my shirt instead. He leans back to allow me space to pull the fabric over my head. He hungrily drags his eyes all over my breasts. I nearly chuckle since my black sports bra smashes them into a very unsexy uniboob. There's no way he's enjoying what he sees that much. But perhaps he's overcome with anticipation since he knows what's constricted beneath.

And since making him wait seems cruel, I tug the zipper in front and allow the spandex to pop open. My breasts spill out, and the erection pressed between us stiffens even more.

Silence hangs in the air. Even Hudson's breathing has stopped, and I can't help but giggle as he surveys my exposed skin.

"Fucking hell, Walker," he chokes out, finding his breath, which stutters shallowly. "They're even better up close."

I laugh. He does too. It's like we both can't believe this is real life. That we're actually coming together after all this time ragging on each other.

"Are you sure?" Hudson asks me, even as he leans down and lightly circles my nipple with the tip of his tongue. The barely there touch floods me with arousal, and I use every ounce of leverage I have to grind against his cock.

"About what?" I absently gasp.

"This. What we're about to do." He shifts to my other breast and teases with the same maddeningly soft touch.

I'm trying to switch off my brain, but he's keeping me checked in. It's frustrating because all I want is to stop thinking. Lose myself. Welcome him across my threshold without giving real consideration to the moral dissonance between us.

But perhaps I should be grateful for his diligence. His persistence is noble. I can tell he's virtuously seeking emphatic consent while also helping me discover if I'll regret our actions by the light of day.

It's unnecessary, though. Because the moment I turned the doorknob to lead us into the dark, I had already decided to let him in.

I palm both sides of his face and lift to catch his eyes. The way he looks at me is indescribable. Like I'm beautiful and sexy and all he's ever wanted. Maybe I am, maybe I'm not, but I'm soaked either way.

"Please fuck me, Hudson Pratt."

Chapter Thirty

Leilani

My words sink in, and Hudson's eyes flash instantly from reverence to combustible desire. He slams his lips hard against mine, pressing me wide for sweeping thrusts of his tongue. He devours me, and I'm too wrapped up in his onslaught to care about the rough wooden planks wreaking havoc on my bare back.

"Stand up," he grunts at me.

I unhook my ankles from behind him and lower my feet to the ground.

"Good girl," he purrs, and I can't keep the grimace from flashing across my face. Understanding dawns. "That's right. Praise isn't your kink."

"It's not," I barely utter, because he's sliding his hands down the front of my shorts and I can't think straight. Not while he skims my clit over the fabric of my panties. Not while he traces the edges. And definitely not while he pulls the lace aside.

"You finally going to tell me what it is?" he growls at my neck. Teeth gently nipping, dragging across my collarbone.

I shake my head. His fingers slick along my seam, and I pant heavily, bracing for him to slide in. But he doesn't. Instead, he releases the fabric back over my pussy and the rush of disappointment is overwhelming. I grab his wrist so he doesn't have the chance to remove it from my shorts altogether.

"Oh, Walker. At least give me a little hint," he croons. His free hand pinches my nipple, which tightens beneath his attention. "I'll play out anything you want."

I believe him. I believe that I could tell him I'd want to have sex in the middle of the field with all the campers watching and he'd find a way to grant the fantasy. The only challenge is that what I like leaves me vulnerable. And while I want to trust Hudson, there's a sliver of me that still doesn't.

That may never.

Still, I can't help my eyes darting down to the front of his hoodie. He follows my glance and grins.

"You want to wear it?" he asks.

I bite my lip and shake my head, chuckling.

Something dawns on his face, and he frees my nipple. I watch lustfully as he grasps one end of the string looped through the hood of his sweatshirt and pulls. My grip relaxes on his wrist so he can remove his other hand from my pants. For a moment, my body feels the chill in the thin space between us.

But then he looks up at me, holding one end of the cord in each hand and a delicious heat zips between my legs.

"Would you like me to tie you up, Walker?"

I nod.

"Hmm?" He turns his ear toward me. "I'm sorry. I didn't catch that."

This is the moment—the point where I decide whether to trust my camp nemesis or walk out of this shack. It's now or never. The point of reckoning.

I hold out my hands, wrists crossed over each other. My chin is dipped low as I look up through my lashes at him. I can't hide the shudder in my voice. "I want you to bind my wrists."

Hudson cups my jaw with both hands and stares into my eyes. He presses his words deep into my consciousness so I know they're genuine. "You will be safe, Leilani," he vows.

And somehow, I believe him.

His kiss is tender, and I know he's taking my vulnerability with all seriousness. I'm eased in that moment. But then I'm alight with anticipation.

He pulls back and winds the string around my wrists in expert fashion. He's either done this before or was a sailor in a past life. The knots are just right, as is the tightness of the bind. It pinches, but in the right way, in the right places. Moisture floods my panties as he kisses my wrists and asks, "There now, how is that?"

"Perfect."

He glances around the little room, likely deciding where and how he wants me and grins when he spots the little stool.

"Stay here," he commands and steps away. In a blink the stool is in his hands, but he stops when we both hear a little thump. He bends down to pick up something that's either fallen or been knocked over. "Did you set this up?"

His question is confusing until he holds out an open condom box with one remaining packet. And I laugh. Barely managing to say, "Bianca and Eddie were in here this morning. They must have forgotten it."

"Or stashed it for a future round." He's chuckling too.

"Either way, it's our gain."

"Yes," Hudson says. Then he sets down the stool and drops the little box next to it. "Now turn around, bend over, and grip the stool."

Chapter Thirty-One

Hudson

I can't tell in the darkness, but I'd bet my life that Leilani's cheeks flush a pretty pink as I tell her to bend over. My cock strains against the zipper of my jeans and I long to have them off. Long to finally fuck my camp crush until she can't walk straight. She's such a strong, commanding woman that the sight of her tied wrists has me throbbing. Especially knowing that the cord that binds her came from *my* hoodie. It's foolish, but I almost feel a heightened sense of possession over her as a result.

My heart slams into my chest at an alarming rate as she does what I tell her to do, and I find myself staring at her heart-shaped ass a little too long. I palm my dick through my pants to get a hint of relief only to realize that won't happen until I come inside of her.

I step forward and run a hand over each cheek and then

grip the top of her shorts. Inch by agonizing inch, I pull them down. Revealing soft skin and glimpsing her panty-clad pussy in the space where her ass meets the backs of her thighs. Soon, denim bunches at her ankles, settled atop her sneakers, which are staying on, by the way.

Goose bumps wash over her legs as I skim my hands up her calves, tickling over the backs of her knees, pressing between her thighs. She's so wet that the strip of lace is soaked through. I play with her, tracing, patting, lightly pinching as she squirms and gasps and begs me for more.

I stand back up and grip the waistband of her thong.

"Want me to remove these?" I ask, fisting the delicate lace.

"Yes," she says with a lusty little hiccup.

I don't delay. With a sharp pull, the fabric rips. I move to the other hip and do the same before sinking down to my knees. Kneeling before her, my eyes are trained on her as I peel the fabric away and reveal her smooth, aching pussy.

"Spread your legs, Walker."

"My shorts are in the way," she groans, shimmying as though seeking my touch.

"Make it work," I command, gripping each ankle, inching them apart. "Good. Now arch your back downward for me."

She does, spreading so I have better access. My hands glide up until I can settle a thumb on either side of her dripping sex. Even in the dark I can see how pink she is, how inviting. I can't hold out any longer.

Her wail is so loud when I drag my tongue from clit to

ass that I'm worried someone will come running to her rescue.

"Shhh," I hush her gently, ensuring the puff of air lands where she's so exposed. "Unless you want to get caught."

"Nooooooo." Her word turns to a groan as I go in for another taste. "That's not . . . part . . . of my—oh god, yes."

"Not part of your fantasy?" I finish her sentence.

"Yeah," she says breathlessly, knees shuddering.

I settle back on my haunches to see the soaked sight of her. My dick pulses, making it clear that I'm not capable of holding off for much longer if this continues. I dismiss the warning because I need to make her come.

My brain chimes in next, reminding me that someone could, in fact, find us at any moment. We have limited time, and I still have an official date to win. Though at this point, my guess is she'd still let me take her out even if *Hudson Sucks* claims the trophy.

"Hudson?" she whispers.

"Sorry," I say, leaning in and dusting a light kiss on the back of her thigh. "I'm back. Just thinking I won't have enough time to do all the things I want to do to you. Had to consider what's most important."

I kiss her other thigh as she asks, "What'd you decide?"

"First," I pause, and lean in for a lingering suck of her clit. I wait until her moan quiets then pull back. "I need to get you off."

She is positively shaking. I take it all in while sliding a finger deep into her. She wails, primal and free, not bothering to temper her enjoyment of my touch, which only urges me on. Soon, I'm fingering her with a singular goal in mind. Curling and pressing just so, aiming for that spot that's likely to have her clenching and dripping down my palm. I find her clit with the thumb of my other hand, rapidly teasing back and forth. Her body tenses, *every inch* of her tenses and I know she's close.

"Tell me how to break you, Leilani," I beg against her hip. The need to give her explosive pleasure takes over my will for anything else. Suddenly, her orgasm is the only thing that will keep me alive. As though it will wash away all of my sins and lead to my salvation.

"Keep going," she pants between moans. "Only more. Faster. Harder."

And so I obey. She's the one bound, but I am her willing captive.

In moments, she comes undone. Shaking. Clenching. Crying out with all the most vulgar words. At the height of her release is when I finally snatch the condom from the little box our friends left behind. I plant a kiss on one of her ass cheeks and stand.

My clanking buckle and zipper fill the tight little building with obscene tension. I release my cock from the constriction of my jeans. I don't even bother pulling them down. They settle right below my sack and I couldn't give a shit.

Rolling on the condom, grabbing Leilani's hips, and squaring up with her dripping pussy is all I can focus on. She's still writhing, clearly aching for more to coax the rest of the orgasm out of her.

And then, I'm sliding into her tight, clenching hold. She

pulses madly around me as we groan in agonizing bliss. She doesn't let me catch my breath; instead, she rocks against me. Forcing me to stand my ground behind her so she doesn't knock me back. She's aiming to reach that high again and I'm more than happy to feed into her greedy demands.

"Fuck me, Pratt," she growls at me, before adding a commanding, "Hard."

My fingertips dig into her hips as I ram into her over and over. I feel her stretch with each punishing thrust. Between our moans and heavy breath, the wet noises of me fucking her fill the room. It's hot. Vulgar. And drugging me in a way that's sure to leave me hungover tomorrow.

The little stool she's braced on scrapes against the floorboards with each thrust until it's pressed against the wall.

"Stand up," I bark and I don't give her the chance to comply before my hand settles on her throat to get her in the upright position myself. Her back is pressed against my front now, hand still encircling her neck. "Touch yourself. Play with your clit until you come again."

She nods and does what I tell her to all while I rail her from behind. And it's minutes, maybe less, before she lets out a broken cry. And that's when I stop holding back and drain myself in her with a rumbling growl. Black spots pepper my vision as pleasure pulses the length of my cock. My sack pulls up tight, ensuring there's nothing left of me to give. I'm pressed as deeply as I can go and can feel her gently sweep her clit as she comes down from bliss alongside me.

Our shouts of ecstasy have subsided. Left is our breath and the heavy scent of sex in the muggy air. I nuzzle her neck, and she arches back against me with a satisfied shiver. I reach around her and untie the string from around her wrists. There's barely a mark, but I gently massage where she was bound regardless.

After a moment, she shakes my hands away.

"Thanks, I needed that," she says with a sexy little sigh.

Chapter Thirty-Two

Hudson

I'm a snuggler. Always have been. There's no shame in it. Something about holding a woman in my arms after slipping out of her feels like the icing on the cake. We get to ride the oxytocin wave together, bask in its shine until it's time to return to the real world. The moments following sex can forge a bond—one I'd very much like to experience with Leilani Walker.

Which is why when she shifts away and pulls up her denim cutoffs, I'm left with a cold emptiness. The hint of connectedness we experienced dissolves and settles among the dust in the little pump house.

I consider asking her to wait a moment, but that drifts away too. Despite the four walls of the tiny shack, we're still pretty exposed.

While she finishes dressing, I take a moment to remove

the condom and toss it in the empty box, then I rebutton my jeans. She hasn't faced me yet. So naturally, the nagging worry that she regrets what we did seeps in with abandon. I watch as she scans the floor, walls, even the ceiling in an effort to look anywhere but at me.

It isn't until she flips the little stool, mumbling to herself, that I realize she's looking for something specific.

And I know what it is.

"What are you doing?" I ask, playing dumb and enjoying the view as she bends over.

"Dropped something," she lies unconvincingly.

"Want help?"

"Nope."

Instead of pressing her, I cross my arms, lean my shoulder against the wall, and watch. The more she searches, the more agitated she gets. Her desperation takes full form as she jumps to look on top of one of the water tanks.

Dropped something, my ass.

"Walker."

"Pratt," she replies with a huff.

"Is this what you dropped?"

She spins around and faces me. When her eyes land on the crumpled orange plastic dangling from my fingers, they narrow accusingly.

"Where did you get that?" she snaps, closing the short distance between us.

"I found it," I say plainly.

"When?" I jerk the flag up and out of her reach as she lunges for it. "Where?"

"Rolled up and tucked in the condom box." I wrap an arm around her waist to keep her from jumping again. "You were a little too busy being tied up and bent over to notice."

I lean in to kiss her, but she pushes out of my arms and steps back. I'm starting to think she's actually agitated about the flag beyond her normal competitive bent.

Soon, she steps forward again and wags a finger in my face. "You knew it was here."

Not loving this new energy of hers—especially so soon after I'd just fucked her silly—I somehow manage to maintain my cool. Externally, that is. Because inside, I'm a riot of confusion, worry, and anxiety. It's like me finding this flag is a personal affront to her, and I can't for the life of me understand why. "I didn't originally. But you following me and acting all weird tipped me off."

"You're sure Eddie didn't tell you?" she asks, cheeks flushed now from being upset rather than turned on. I hate the shift. I truly thought the afterglow cease-fire would have lingered a bit longer than this.

"Like I already said," I explain, saying each word as clearly and carefully as I can. "I've barely seen Eddie all week. Wednesday was the last day we talked, and even that wasn't much because he seemed a little mopey."

"Fine." She visibly deflates but doesn't seem satisfied.

"Based on the third degree, I assume you knew about it, though." I don't care much but playfully accusing her seems justified.

She crosses her arms and lifts her chin.

"Leilani Walker," I draw out her name, low and scolding.

Her little shiver is delicious, and I seriously consider suggesting another round, this time in one of our bunks.

"I knew about it." She shrugs and drops her arms. "Bianca crashed breakfast this morning and told me and Mel that she and Eddie found it."

"Ah, so you were cheating." Again, I don't care if she was, but messing with her about it is satisfying my inner pest.

"I don't cheat," she snaps. Her eyes are blazing narrow slits that I half expect will shoot laser beams at any moment. "I wasn't going to go after this flag. Ask Mel. She was there when I told Bianca I didn't want to win that way. That I wanted to win fair and square."

"I believe you," I assure. She tracks the flag as I hold up both hands to calm her, and I struggle to ignore the sinking sensation in my chest.

Look, I'm not one of those guys who gets hooked on a woman the first time we have sex. Like I said, I enjoy a good cuddle, but I'm able to tell the difference between just pleasure and real intimacy. But this time around, with Leilani, I'm feeling something deeper than I ever have. It's not love, let's be clear about that; we don't know or trust each other enough for that. But I'd be a fool to ignore the intensity of what we shared. Like it could be something so much more than a one-week-per-year showdown with someone I find sexy as hell.

But I have no clue if she's on the same page.

Which is precisely why I ask, "Do you still want to? Win, I mean?"

"Of course." No hesitation.

"So you won't have to go out with me?" I can't seem to find my usual volume, and the words feel gritty like sand on my tongue. "So that I never come back to camp?"

Leilani blinks a few times like she's thinking it over to give me her honest thoughts. Something's battling inside of her, but I'm afraid of what I'll find if I dig deeper. That this was all a meaningless hookup to her while I'm sitting here like a chump praying that she'll go all in with me. Finally, she sighs pensively. "Right."

"Right," I repeat, raising my hand to massage the space between my eyes. I hold the flag out to her. "You should take this."

She shakes her head. "You found it."

I make space for her as she walks around me. Three short steps and she's at the door. It creaks as noisily as it did when we entered the structure a short time ago. We'll be seeing each other again in a matter of twenty minutes when the game ends, but things have changed. Drastically. And as she leaves, I'm wondering if what we just shared was a bad idea.

I snatch the condom box because I hate leaving any place worse off than I found it. Strolling down the trail that leads back to our team baskets, I come to a garbage can. Without hesitation, I crumple up the bright orange flag, tuck it into the box, and throw it away.

Chapter Thirty-Three

Leilani

P*eeeeeeep.*

Counselor Clark wails on the whistle that hangs around his neck, signifying the end of the multi-flag capture. My entire team is present, some bent over and gasping for air. Albert is lying prone in the dirt, looking like he's approaching death's door. I press on a fake smile and high five each member, telling them what a great job they did, while also avoiding Hudson's forlorn stare.

He might think I do, but I don't regret what we did in the pump house. Our chemistry was through the roof; I've never come that hard in my life. And while I'd love an encore, I'm still not convinced that he and I would be a good fit in general.

I trusted him enough to be vulnerable.

I trusted him enough to fuck.

But I don't think I can trust him to put me first when we're out in the real world, and that's where I draw the line.

Astrid steps forward to address the group, appearing less bubbly than usual. Her smile is forced and her shoulders slumped. An instant wave of protectiveness comes over me as I wonder who's been a dick to my favorite camp counselor.

"As usual," she calls out, "we'll count the flags tonight and announce the winners at closing ceremonies tomorrow morning after breakfast. In the meantime, grab yourself some pizza. There are beers and ciders in the big red buckets. Enjoy the foam party and your last night at Evergreen Adventure Camp!"

She and Clark each grab a basket of flags and head to the mess hall as the crowd erupts in celebration and Montell Jordan's "This is How We Do It" blares through the speakers at the perimeter of the large field.

"Good hustle, everyone," I hear Hudson shout to his team over the noise. "I think we have a pretty good chance of being declared the winners this year."

He catches me watching him and smiles, though this time there isn't a hint of mocking or scorn. The dynamic we've shared for the last five summers is irrevocably changed. I no longer feel a fiery rage when I look at him. Our interaction in the pump house has tempered that. We may be on opposing teams, but one thing is clear: our rivalry is over. This saddens me, but I push away the urge to mourn the shift. Now is not the time.

"Chick, you look wrecked," Bianca says bluntly, pulling me out of my mope.

She and Mel approach, both looking me up and down, making their assessments.

"I'm that bad, huh?" I ask, reaching for my hair and finding my ponytail all out of sorts.

"Like you've been ridden hard and put away wet, right, Mel?" Bee elbows our friend's side. Mel swats at Bianca.

"Don't listen to her. You're lovely as always," she croons.

"Thanks, *Mom*," I say, rolling my eyes and chuckling.

Either Mel doesn't detect the sarcasm or she does but can discern the genuine appreciation beneath it. She moves in for a hug, squeezing the life out of me in a way I've grown accustomed. I settle into the rib-popping embrace and giggle as Bianca sidles up and nudges her way in.

We group hug for a while, none of us wanting to be the first to disentangle from the comfort. Until my stomach growls like a petulant child.

Melody pulls back and nods toward the line of campers waiting for pizza. "I'm loving the cuddle, but that sound tells me we have about five minutes to feed her before hangry Leilani crashes the party."

"Yeah," Bianca agrees. "I could use a bite too."

"Come on," I say, looping my arms through each of theirs and tug them toward the end of the line. "Let's stuff ourselves silly then dance 'till we drop. It's our last night here. I wanna make it count."

Chapter Thirty-Four

Hudson

"What aren't you telling us, Edward?" Charles asks. His eyes don't leave our friend even as Eddie stuffs half a slice of pepperoni pizza in his mouth to keep from answering.

The three of us sit together in mismatched Adirondack chairs on the mess hall porch. It's the last night of camp, and capture the flag is officially done, which means it's time for the late-night pizza feed. The annual foam party is already in full swing. Many of the campers shovel their slices and dive into the bubbles with the wild abandon of kindergartners at . . . well . . . a foam party.

Typically, Charles and I mow down on pizza and watch the chaos from a safe distance. This time around, we're graced with Eddie's presence. Though he looks exactly how I feel.

Glum.

Disappointed.

And a little bit antsy.

I'm about to ask if he's upset because Leilani and I used his last condom in the pump house, but Charles starts first.

"Did Bee finally dump your ass?" He wipes his face with a napkin, tosses it onto his empty plate, and leans back with a groan. "Found someone else to play with at camp?"

"No," Eddie grumbles through chews. He stabs Charles with a death glare and takes a swig of beer.

"You sure about that?" We follow Charles's line of sight out to the mass of partiers wearing glow bracelets and shirts that illuminate under all the black lights. It's dark, yet plain as day we can see Bianca tugging some guy into the foam. But not before she darts a scowl up to where we sit.

I let out a low whistle. "Kendrick? Yikes, man. Of all the guys to lose out to."

"She's trying to get back at me," Eddie explains, dropping his half-eaten pizza on his plate before casting it aside on one of the empty chairs.

Charles and I share a meaningful look. For as long as we've both known him, our friend has always been a bottom-less pit when it comes to food. We joke that he has two empty legs that just won't fill. He's the guy who eats the pizza crust we didn't finish, not the guy who calls it quits after a slice and a half. This character shift can only mean one thing.

He's screwed the pooch.

"What did you do?" I ask, handing him my unopened

beer as he swallows the final drops of his. He accepts it, pops the tab, and gulps heartily.

"I ended things with her."

"What?!" Our twin shrieks draw attention from a nearby cluster of campers.

"You ended things?" Charles presses.

"I had to." Eddie looks so deflated. No crooked grin. No twinkle in his eye. I never knew he could slump his shoulders that much.

"Why?" I demand. "What you've got with Bee has been going on for years. What changed?"

He shrugs, even while his head hangs pathetically. "I can't keep this up."

"And carb loading wasn't an option? Downing a couple of energy drinks beforehand?" I'm trying desperately to lighten the mood, but a dirty look from Charles has me changing tactics. "What can't you keep up?"

"I love her." Eddie lifts his head and there are honest to god tears welling in the corners. "This one-week-a-year hookup isn't enough for me anymore. I need more. So, I told her either we give this a chance for real or we end it for good."

"And I'm guessing she went with option two?" Charles asks.

"Kind of." He polishes off the rest of his beer and crushes the can against the arm of his chair. "Said she 'doesn't do relationships' or some bullshit like that. Asked me why I'd want to ruin a good thing. Look, I'm not one of those guys that's going to push. Either she wants me or she doesn't. She can't only have my dick, ya know? So, I ended it."

By this point, he's dropped his face into his hands and lets out a miserable groan.

Charles reaches over and pats him on the back. "You did the right thing."

"How can you say that?" No one misses the higher-than-normal octave my voice hits. After a subtle throat clearing I try again. "He's just supposed to let her walk away?"

"As opposed to what, chasing her down and begging her to be with him?"

"If that's what it takes. All he needs is a chance to show her." I'm breathing heavily, all worked up. "Maybe she'd change her mind if she spent some time with him outside of this place. She'd see how good they could be. How much work he's put into being a better version of himself. That he's *changed* and isn't the same douchebag she met four years ago."

This time, it's Charles and Eddie's turn to share a look.

"What?" I say defensively.

Eddie's forlorn chuckle has me scowling. "Someone's projecting."

"I'm not projecting. It just sucks that Bianca won't give you a chance."

"And this has nothing to do with the bet you and Leilani made about her going out on a date with you? It has nothing to do with you 'secretly' pining over her more and more over the last four years?" Charles props an ankle on his knee to retie his sneaker. "Both of you are so hopeless. Thank god one of us is a married man and can see around the blinders."

"I'm dying to hear your wisdom, oh wedded one," I snap,

knowing full well what Charles is about to tell us. But for once I want my friend to leave me alone to stew in my delusions.

Don't I?

Or would I rather someone slap me across the face and tell me to act like a grown man?

"Eddie," Charles begins. "You made the right call. If you're looking to protect your heart, you have to maintain those boundaries. Prolonging a situation that only brings you occasional joy is an absolute waste of your time. And you—" He turns and points a finger in my face. He's making the switch from good cop to bad cop, and I'm not exactly thrilled to be on the receiving end. "Can you please get your head out of your ass?"

"Excuse me?"

"It's crammed so far up there you can't see through all your own bullshit."

"Gross, dude," Eddie mumbles, and I'm inclined to agree.

Our friend continues, though. He's all fired up, ready to tell me my business and all I'm thinking is that I hope it gives me some kind of clarity. I'm desperate for it.

"You and Leilani have been at each other's throats since the moment you met and started bragging about your new promotion, and how you were better than your girlfriend, blah blah blah. You were a money-hungry douchebag, and frankly I don't blame her for hating you."

"Ouch." I feign hurt. Ok fine, I pretend to feign hurt because it does actually cut me a little.

"Were, Hudson," Charles clarifies. "You *were* a money-hungry douchebag. But you've come a long way since then. Literally knocked on death's door and saw where your skewed priorities would lead you. It's been no picnic, but you've changed. You walked away from a job that was literally killing you and never looked back. You spend your time trying to make amends to people you've wronged. You've become someone that matches the real you I met back in middle school. And if Leilani had met you this week, I'm sure she would have been all over you. But she still has the aftertaste of the old you in her mouth and your stupid-ass bet doesn't help that."

I hear what he's saying, and I know he's right. There's no denying the damage done from when I first met Leilani. First impressions are nearly impossible to overcome, and I've done nothing since then but reinforce her beliefs about me.

Which leaves me with only one path forward.

I jet to my feet and turn toward the mass of foam and gyrating bodies. It glows under the black lights and practically vibrates with each thump of bass.

"Where are you going?" Charles asks, but something tells me he has a pretty good idea.

"To show Leilani that I've changed."

Chapter Thirty-Five

Leilani

Someone once said dancing your face off was the best medicine when your heart is all out of sorts. While it's not exactly healing anything, all this twirling, dipping, and laughing with Mel sure is boosting my spirits. Bubbles and sweat coat my body as I shake my ass to Shakira. Multicolored glow stick flashes bounce off the walls of fluffy white that surround us. Periodically, someone comes crashing through the barrier. Some campers pass on through while others stay and dance with us a bit.

For the first time all week, simple joy washes over me. I have Melody to thank for that. I think about the shit she's been through with her divorce and the work she's done to heal herself and can't help but be in awe of her resilience. She's full of renewed vitality and I'm not ashamed at how greedily I soak it all in. There's no way of knowing how much this place contributed to the shift—I'm pretty sure most of it results from the work she's been doing on herself prior to our vacation—but I'm certain camp has helped galvanize her reassembled pieces.

Mel grabs my hands and twirls me around in some fancy swing dance move. She winds me into her chest and spins me back out. The foamy slop causes my hand to slip from her grip and I tumble through the bubbles right into a brick wall. Or maybe it's a huge tree trunk, because intense wafts of pine and cedar slap me around a little.

When did we dance to the edge of the field?

It's not until two giant meat claws grip my shoulders that I realize I've run into a large flannel-clad man with an iconic beard.

"Uh, Russell, right?" I shout at the brute over the pounding music.

He nods with a grunt while peeling me from his soaking wet shirt and taking a step back. It's incredible how different he is from his grandparents. Hank and Jolly always exude joy and love and brightness, but this guy . . .

He's the walking embodiment of a storm cloud.

"Sorry for barreling into you like that. My friend spun me and lost her hold on my hand. The bubbles are slippery." I scoop a clump and toss it into the air.

Russell's eyes dart everywhere but at me. He's searching for something.

Or someone.

The least I can do is offer my services after slamming into him a minute ago. "Can I help you with—"

"You know Astrid?" he interrupts.

"Sure. We all know Astrid."

His eyes zero in on me as I repeat her name like the syllables are a homing beacon. He steps forward, and I have no choice but to retreat in kind. I'm not scared of him, but this dude is massive.

"Where?" he demands.

"Where what?"

He shakes his head and fiddles with his beard like he's trying to organize his thoughts before speaking again.

"Have you seen Astrid?" He says her name again with such reverence and something pinches in my heart.

"Not since she left to count the flags before the party," I shout.

Just then, Mel barrels through the foamy wall to my right, missing me by mere inches.

"There you are," she laughs. "Sorry about flinging you into the abyss. Don't know my own strength."

She notices Russell and gives him a little wave.

"He's looking for Astrid," I explain. To which Mel nods.

"Have you seen her?" Desperation mars his words.

Mel nods. "Yeah, I saw her head toward Heartbreak Lake earlier."

"When?" Russell asks, stepping in toward us.

I step back again, but Mel holds her ground. She even dons a little smile and places a hand on his hairy forearm. "Ten minutes or so."

His mustache twitches with a brief smile of thanks, and then Russell takes off. As he plows through the foam, he leaves a massive tunnel in his wake. A few partiers poke their heads in to investigate then enter the space to dance and twirl in the opening.

I turn to Mel, unable to contain my laughter. "I swear, camp isn't usually this . . . weird."

"I like it," she calls back. "This has been the perfect week. Exactly what I need."

This time, it's my turn to pull her in for a crushing hug.

"Leilani." Hudson appears beside us. He glances between Mel and me. "Can I steal you for a minute?"

"I don't want to ditch Mel," I respond, twining my fingers with my friend's. She squeezes my hand tightly and I imagine her transferring some of her unending strength to me. Her love and support fill me. Comfort me.

Just as quickly, she lets go and nudges me with her shoulder.

"Go," she insists. "I'll be fine without you."

"But I don't want to abandon you—"

"Hush," she demands, placing her hands on her hips and leaning toward me in a way that's supposed to be menacing in an *I'm-your-mom-and-you'll-do-as-you're-told* sort of way. "Go. I'll dance for a bit then call it a night."

Mel winks at us. Then she turns and disappears into the glowing, pulsing mass of bubbles. At the same time, Hudson tugs gently on my hand, leading me out of the chaos and toward the edge of the tree line.

I marvel at the warmth of his large hand encircling mine. Something about it feels stabilizing. Correct.

We weave through the woods along one of the many dirt paths until we reach a wooden bench.

And his hand slips from mine.

The sense of loss is jarring, until I remind myself of who I'm here with and who we are to each other. The buzz of beer and foam and fun evaporates and suddenly I'm sober.

"What do you need to talk to me about?" I ask, crossing my arms to combat the chill crawling up my shoulders. The sun has long since dipped behind the surrounding mountains, and while the heat from the day lingers, a shiver ripples down my spine anyway.

Hudson lowers to the bench and pats the planks beside him, asking me to sit. I make no move to comply until a ragged, "Please, Leilani" rumbles through his lips.

I sigh deeply, drop my arms, but eventually stalk to settle in beside him.

"Well?" I ask, insisting he proceed with whatever this is.

"I figured we're long overdue for a heart-to-heart."

Chapter Thirty-Six

Hudson

I'd laugh at the way Leilani's mouth silently gapes open and shut if it weren't for the trauma I'm about to unload on her. I consider forging ahead without her saying anything, but ultimately decide to wait for some kind of response.

Finally, she says, "Of all the things, this is the last I'd expect on my bingo card."

"Really?" I say skeptically, scrunching my face in mild judgment. "Compared to you flashing me, the shower incident, and us having sex in the pump house, a meaningful conversation is unexpected?"

She nods and I'm thrown off guard.

"The first one was all strategy," she begins, swatting her hand through the air as though wafting away some annoying bug. "You're not the first person I've flashed, Hudson Pratt. They're just boobs."

Even as she says it I glance down at her chest because how could I not? "Nothing on you is 'just anything'."

She ignores my declaration. "And then the shower incident was . . ."

"Hot?" I offer as she trails off thinking for the right description.

Her cheeks flush as she looks down at her shoes. This coy innocence is so unlike her, and it throws me a little. She must catch herself in the act, so near flirting, because her head snaps up and she presses her lips into a deep scowl.

"It was a game of chicken. Or an unspoken dare. Was it hot? Sure. I'm alive aren't I? A woman would have to be dead to disagree, but it didn't mean anything. And the sex?"

"The sex," I parrot as my heart thumps deep in my chest. Each beat signals that it's working overtime, but I'm grateful for it working at all.

"The sex was great."

"But?" Because I know there's a but coming.

"No but. That's it. The sex was great." Her words are exactly what I want to hear, but her bleak tone says something altogether different.

"Come on, Walker. Don't start caring about my feelings all of a sudden," I say, chuckling half-heartedly.

"Ok, fine." She rolls her eyes and sighs deeply. "But that's where it all ends."

"Which means I have nothing left to lose." And I believe that.

"Care to elaborate?" she asks snottily.

"Only if you're not a brat about it."

Her mouth flops open in shock but it's short-lived. She knows it's true. At least with me she's bratty. So she sits up straight and mimes locking her lips.

Here goes nothing.

"Six months ago, I had a heart attack," I begin.

"Ok, sure. You had a heart attack at forty-two," Leilani scoffs. But when I wait patiently, not saying anything more, something clicks in her. She suddenly believes me. "You had a heart attack at *forty-two*?!"

I nod.

"What the hell, Hudson?" she sputters. "How?"

"Stress. Pure, intense, panic-inducing stress."

"From your super awesome job?" she asks sarcastically.

"Exactly that."

Her voice softens. "Does Charles know?"

"Yeah. He and Aaron insisted I recover in their guest bedroom."

"So, what happened?"

"It was the worst and scariest day of my life," I begin, sighing deeply. "I was meeting with the exec team one night —we all stuck around to prep the earnings presentation for the board. My boss was railing me because my team underperformed that quarter by two percent. A measly two percent. Our goals were already stupidly high quarter after quarter, but our growth was deemed 'subpar' in his opinion." I wince as I remember the bulge of that old bastard's eyes, the reddening of his face as he screamed at me. He'd started on one side of the table but his rage-fueled haze had him stepping around to stand in front of my chair. He leaned over me, finger and spittle in my face as he told me what a loser I was. A waste of space that couldn't motivate a team of monkeys to fling their own shit. The smell of old cheesesteak and cigarette smoke wafted off of him like some over-applied cologne. The stench made me nauseated, turned my stomach so badly that I thought I might hurl right on his fancy fucking loafers.

"It was eight p.m. on the dot," I continue, urging my heart to calm down. It beats so violently as I imagine myself back in that situation. But I'm not there. I'm somewhere infinitely better but almost as nerve-racking. With Leilani. Spilling my guts. "That's when a pinching sensation worked its way along my left arm. I remember because it pulled all my focus. I scanned my arm from shoulder to wrist and spotted the time on my watch. Anyways, I shook it out, trying to relieve the nagging twinge. But it became more and more painful. Eventually, my boss pulled back and asked me 'what the fuck my problem was' right as my chest started constricting. I couldn't breathe. Couldn't say anything because I was dumbstruck."

"You're young. And fit." Her brain is working overtime to compute the likelihood of this. I can tell because it's exactly how I responded when the doctors explained the situation to me. "I've seen you naked, Pratt. You're no slouch."

My chest puffs up at her inadvertent compliment.

I watch as she absorbs my words. Her adorable nose is scrunched and her eyebrows press together so a little line deepens between them. The urge to trail a finger down the bridge of her nose in order to relax her expression flits past.

I'm not sure how she'd react if I touched her right now, so I opt to add a little space.

"My dad died young," I say, rising to my feet. I snag a leaf off a nearby bush and idly tear it apart. Once all the bits have fallen to the dirt, I stuff my hands in my pockets. "He was barely fifty before heart disease took him. I'd watched him neglect his body by going from work to the couch all my life. The man ate whatever junk tasted good and washed it down with half a dozen beers. I was determined to live a different life. Took care of my body to live a *longer* life. But the type of work I chose wreaked its own havoc. Not just on my body, but on who I was. The stress and pressure came with certain perks, and I scooped them up like a greedy bastard not noticing if it meant selling my soul in the process."

"Wait," Leilani cut in. "You're telling me you didn't *notice* your job was turning you into an asshole?"

"I guess," I say with a weak shrug.

She hops to her feet and marches over to face me. Her hand settles on my arm and the skin beneath it tingles in response. "Look, I'm sorry for what happened to you. Dealing with a heart attack must have been . . . terrifying. But there's no way you didn't notice how you acted. How you talked to people, or about people for that matter. Like at that first campfire, when you were talking shit about your long-term girlfriend?"

Jessica.

In the end, I treated her like she was disposable. Like I was headed for the high life and all she did was drag me down. I remember the look of pure heartbreak when I

216

returned home from that first week of camp and told her we were over.

She deserved so much more from me. Which is precisely what I told her when I begged her to have coffee with me a few months ago. She sat patiently across from me, cool as a cucumber, while I apologized. I rambled on for ten solid minutes about how much of a dirtbag I'd been. Her sweet smile ripped my heart in two, and her forgiveness felt like shards of glass under my skin. Because I didn't deserve it. I deserved to have her latte thrown in my face or a hearty slap while she calls me a bastard.

"I was an insufferable ass, wasn't I?"

"Were?" she teases and drops her hand to her side. My arm is cold where she no longer touches me.

"I'm sorry for who I've been, Leilani Walker. The last six months, I've been working hard on myself. Trying to change back into the version I lost."

"Thank you for telling me, but you don't owe me anything, Hudson Pratt." The teasing use of my full name nearly masks her sadness.

Nearly.

She pauses. Waits for me to say something. Anything. But I don't. I'm a chicken. A coward who chokes on the urge to do the right thing and actually show her how I've changed. I've lived a long time on my own terms; everyone else's wishes be damned. And for a moment, I consider that maybe I can continue to do so and still come out with a clean slate.

My silence must tell her all she needs to know because

Leilani turns and begins down the trail, back to the throng of soapy campers and away from me.

I feel the connection we shared earlier in the pump house slipping away. Who am I kidding? Much of that happened the instant we walked out of the little building. But any chance I have with Leilani lingers out of reach. Like I could charm or beg or reason but nothing would reignite the passion we shared.

But reigniting that burn wasn't the reason I pulled her out here in the first place. And I know deep down that any hope of success can't be on my terms.

Before she's too far, I call to her.

"I'm dropping my stakes of the bet."

Chapter Thirty-Seven

Leilani

I must have misheard him.

It sounded like Hudson Pratt is backing out of our bet.

But that can't be the case. For one, he'd never do that. The Pratt I know would never bruise his ego by admitting defeat before the results were announced. He also wouldn't skip out on a chance to get something he wants. Something he believes he's owed.

For two, he's not the only one with stakes in the game. He can't just unilaterally decide the bet is off. It's not how things work.

Spinning around, I march over to stand face-to-face with him.

"What the hell?" I demand, jabbing him in the chest so hard it hurts my finger a little.

He winces and rubs the spot where I poked him. "That'll leave a pointy bruise."

"You can't drop out of the bet. We shook on it."

"Did we? I don't remember shaking hands."

"Well, we agreed to the terms. We struck an agreement. A gentle . . . gentle-people's agreement."

"A gentle-people's agreement?"

"Whatever, we agreed. A date if you win. You lose your hoodies and never return to camp if I win. It's already been decided." I'm huffy. Though I can't quite decide why. The delusional part of me wants to believe that it has something to do with not getting what I want the most if I win. For Hudson to leave camp and never return. I'd be missing out on the chance to be rid of him for good. To come to camp and enjoy my time without an overshadowing mission to destroy this man. I could still play capture the flag of course. Could even continue being one of the captains. I'd just have a different rival heading up the other team.

Gloom overcomes me; it seeps in through each pore of my body at the thought of battling someone else. The weight of it makes my heart stutter. My knees wobble. My lower lip follows suit until I bite it to mask my reaction. The idea of Hudson no longer being my camp nemesis is crushing, and it throws me.

He hasn't said anything; he only stands there watching. Eyes roaming all over me as though he's seeking some unspoken answer to a question he's afraid to ask.

We stay like this for a while until Hudson steps toward me. He's slow, steady, like if he moves too quickly, he'll spook me and I'll bolt. The toes of his sneakers touch the tips of mine, his hoodie grazing my breasts. Even through my bra and tank top the contact makes my nipples pearl. Inadvertently, I arch my back, pressing onto him and his warmth.

"You're killing me, Walker," he groans.

He snakes a hand around my waist, beneath my shirt. The press of his fingertips into the small of my back has my pulse racing. His hands shake and I can completely relate. I'm shaking too. The hit I had of him earlier this evening satisfied for a moment, but I was itching for another fix the instant I left the pump house.

Hudson Pratt is my illicit substance and I'm not ashamed to admit I'm addicted.

"Good," I murmur even as I graze my lips beneath his jaw.

His chest rumbles. For a second, I think he's growling and it makes me giggle against his neck.

"You're such a brat." His voice is broken, husky. It's taking a lot for him to mind himself. I'm certain he'd shove me against a tree and teach me a lesson if only he'd let go.

"Only to you," I say sweetly, then gasp as he fists my hair and jerks back. I'm forced to look up at him. There's fire in his eyes. A lust that consumes and presses on his thin patience. The hand that has been pressing into my lower back releases. He slides it around my hip and soon it glides up, skimming my ribs and the side of my breast. It finally settles on my jaw, holding me firm. I tremor, my knees are again so weak, but this time for a completely different reason.

I want one final fuck from this man. And then I'll come

to grips with whatever the outcome of our bet is. But first, I need him inside me.

When he drags his thumb over my bottom lip and into my mouth, I know I've got him. Especially as I suck him deeper and swirl the tip with my tongue.

"Goddamnit," Hudson curses violently. He pulls his thumb from my mouth and replaces it with his tongue. His firm lips seal on mine. This kiss is everything I need, yet I know I shouldn't want it. The very notion is cliché, but it fits. Hudson Pratt is the wrong man for me.

And I couldn't care less as my back scrapes against the bark of the nearest tree trunk. The heady scent of pine and warm sap mingles with his sweat and the soapy foam I'd been dancing in for nearly an hour before he pulled me aside to talk.

It all feels like quintessential summer.

Heat lingering long into the night.

The thump of music and dance of laughter that seep through the trees.

A sordid make out session with the hot guy at camp that I have nothing in common with.

Suddenly, it's my first time at camp. Excited for a fun vacation with my friend. I'm reminded of the blinding clarity that launched me into a new state of being. Taking more for myself rather than sitting back and waiting for my fiancé to prioritize me. There was nervousness and sadness when I left at the end of that week, but ultimately I knew in my soul I was making the right decision.

But then I remember exactly what gave me that clarity and grind to a screeching halt.

My first time meeting Hudson.

The same man who has his tongue in my mouth.

The same man who's pressing me up against this pine as he dry humps me into oblivion.

The same man who's on some bullshit soul-searching journey to change when he'll probably drift back to his suits and ties and work obsession before the year is out.

I can't walk myself back into a life where I'm not a priority to my partner.

"Stop," I whisper as I drop my chin and break our kiss.

Hudson freezes. His hand still rests on my jaw with his other forearm braced against the tree above my head. The rise and fall of his chest is choppy, much like mine. His heart taps an erratic rhythm that I can feel between my breasts, one that I mourn as he carefully presses away from me.

The lust in his eyes wanes and it seems that reality has crept back in and sobered him too.

Which sucks.

The horny, carefree part of me wants him to press against me. Descend upon me and pull me back into the hazy arousal.

But the rational chick in the back of my head is much, much louder.

"Sorry, I—" Hudson breaks off. I watch the long line of his throat as he swallows. He's stepped back from me fully now, and I feel chilled as the warm summer breeze tickles past. He clears his throat and adjusts the front of his pants then stuffs his hands into the pockets of his worn hoodie. "It's so easy to get carried away with you."

"I know the feeling," I say, more to myself than to him.

Glancing up, there's no way to miss his blown-out pupils and rosy cheeks.

"Leilani—"

"No," I say before he can offer up whatever platitude feels right to him in this moment. "Wait."

And he does. He stands there with all the patience in the world, simply waiting for me to figure my shit out.

It's fair to say I'm having some kind of momentary existential crisis. But the fact that it's centered around Hudson Pratt is ridiculous. The only remedy is space. I need distance to organize my thoughts.

"I'm going to go," I finally announce, and he doesn't move to stop me as I shift off the tree and return to the dirt path. Even as I back away slowly, he gives no indication that he might follow. He may be still, but his eyes are expectant. "About the bet—"

"It's off," he states.

"Again, why do you get to decide?" I'm still irked at the one-sided decision.

"Because . . . I only want a date with you if you're a willing participant in the process, and—" he shrugs, still making no move toward me. He's let go. I know it even before he continues. "Regardless of the outcome, I won't be coming back to Camp Clandestine."

Chapter Thirty-Eight

Hudson

Sleep does not come.

Not with my bunkmate sawing logs above me like he's a freaking lumberjack. Each shuddering inhale shakes the rickety wooden bed frame, followed by an exhale so high-pitched I expect dogs to howl in the distance.

Even if Lord of the Deviated Septum weren't filling the cabin with his trumpeting call, I'd be awake. I'm still reeling from the events of the day.

From announcing to Leilani that I won't be returning to camp next year.

Or any year after.

Letting her know that I'd only want to go out with her if she wanted the same thing. The last thing I want is to *win* her. She's not some reward that I deserve for a job well-done.

She's a vibrant, stubborn, sexy person, and I'd give almost anything for her to be interested in me beyond some temporary hate-sex situation. When I came to camp this week, I was convinced that I'd take whatever I could get from Leilani Walker.

And now that's not the case.

I want all or nothing.

Even if nothing is the most probable outcome.

Flopping over onto my belly, I groan a few expletives into the ergonomic pillow I brought from home. Either I'm louder than I intended to be or the memory foam isn't as muffling as I expect because a quiet throat clearing catches my attention.

"Sorry," I whisper into the stuffy darkness.

Charles's quiet chuckle ripples through the air. "Can't sleep?"

"Nope."

The wooden slats of his bed groan under his weight as he shifts and descends the bunk ladder. His feet hit the floor and he instantly leans into the bunk below his to shake our friend awake. "Yo, Eddie."

Eddie mumbles a few word salad phrases as though he's deep in some crazy dream and eventually comes to with a groan. "What?"

"Come on, man," Charles murmurs as he settles his feet into his slides. "Hudson needs us. Let's go for a walk."

"Fine, fine."

I crawl out of bed, no need to put on my shoes because, like a heathen, I'd flopped into my bunk without taking anything off after leaving Leilani. My mother would be horrified. We're all as quiet as possible as we tiptoe out of the cabin and onto the porch. Eddie slips into his shoes, which he left outside beside the front door. No one speaks as we follow the crushed gravel path out to the empty fire pit in the center of the semicircle of guys' cabins.

"So?" Charles breaks the silence once we settle into the weathered Adirondack chairs.

"Yeah. What's up?" Eddie adds through an obnoxious yawn.

I shrug. "Couldn't sleep."

Charles drags both hands over his face, scratching at the black stubble along his jaw. "Look, brother. This is my last night away from the twins. And while I miss them and Aaron, I'm also under no delusion that they've moved beyond the waking up and toddling into our room two or three times a night phase since I've been gone. I'd prefer a few more hours of uninterrupted sleep before we leave in the morning, but I'm here as long a you need me. All I ask is you don't waste my time."

He glances over at Eddie, who's fallen back to sleep in the lawn chair between us. I roll my eyes and we bust out laughing.

"I'm sure he's here in spirit," Charles chuckles.

"He's a brave man for falling asleep," I say, shaking my head.

"Feeling the urge for another *Weekend at Bernie's* remake?"

On no less than a dozen occasions, Eddie has passed out

around the two of us and every time, Charles and I pose him in some crazy way and snap pictures. There's even an Instagram page dedicated to our shenanigans. Sometimes there are costumes or other people who help. Over the years we've gotten increasingly more creative, which means it's been increasingly more challenging to top the last.

"Honestly, I don't think I have the bandwidth." I collapse back into my chair and glance up at the starry night. A few wispy clouds mosey by, but besides that, the vast darkness is illuminated by a trillion sparkling lights.

"I figured."

"I cancelled our bet."

He leans forward and props his elbows on his knees. "The one between you and Lei?"

"The very same."

"Hmm." The Adirondack creaks as Charles relaxes back against it.

"I also won't be coming back to camp next year."

I expect outrage or at the very least mild disappointment. This yearly getaway has become a tradition, something all three of us look forward to and talk about during the off months. We count down the days until it kicks off, often sending a reminder that we're "X" number of days away from our carefree camp week.

But all I get is a lackluster, "I figured as much."

Turning slowly in my chair, I eye Charles, who's either stargazing or searching for UFOs. I assumed I'd get a barrage of questions from him. Demands to explain my decision. I didn't expect his calm acceptance.

"And you're cool with that?" I love my buddy. Both of them, even if one falls asleep during our periodic late-night heart-to-hearts.

Charles shrugs again. "I love coming to camp. There's something light and invigorating about an entire week doing dumb kid stuff. No responsibilities. I'm not someone's husband or daddy here—"

"I'm sure there are some who'd *want* you to be their daddy."

"Dude. Crossing a line. I married my best friend twelve years ago and never looked back. Never will look back. But sometimes, I miss out on being me. Being Charles. That's who I get to be here."

"Now I feel like a dick for taking that from you."

"Nah." He snorts, shaking his head. "You're missing the point. It's not this place. It's time away with my second and third best friends."

I scowl and ask, "I'll accept that Aaron's your first, but out of Eddie and me, who's second and who's third?"

"Depends on the day."

This pulls a genuine laugh out of me. One that overtakes me and rubs off on Charles. Our shoulders shake mirthfully until the bout of sleepy giggles tapers away.

"Seriously, though," I urge. I want to make sure I'm not pissing in his cereal by switching up our annual getaway. "You're not upset that I don't want to come back to camp?"

"Nope," he says simply. "As long as we all do something together, I'm cool."

Even as a nagging hint of guilt swirls in my gut, the

warmth of friendship tamps it down. I sit beside my two best friends in the whole world and realize I've got everything I need right here. The concern of going back home and floating aimlessly doesn't constrict my chest in fear like it did a few days ago. I'll figure out something. And in the meantime, I'll keep working on bettering myself.

I may have destroyed my chances of taking Leilani out on a date, but I'm at peace with it because it was the right call. The correct thing to do. I want her to choose me. And no amount of scheming will lead to anything authentic.

She deserves the genuine article. And the only way I can give her that, or any woman in the future for that matter, is to become the best version of myself.

"Ready to take some weird pictures of Eddie?" Charles asks casually.

"What about getting your last few hours of uninterrupted sleep before going home?"

"I'm awake now. Might as well make the best of it," he say with a twinkle in his eye.

"Oh, what the hell. You've convinced me."

"Didn't take much effort."

"Rarely does." I clap my buddy on the back and take hold of Eddie's ankles.

Charles slides his forearms beneath our comatose friend's pits. We lift together and head for the docks in the muggy night. Crickets chirp, leaves rustle in a gentle breeze, and I reminisce over the last four years. It feels right to bow out for good after tomorrow.

But not before I make one final spectacle of myself. Hey, it's my last year at Camp Clandestine. Might as well go out in a blaze of glory.

Chapter Thirty-Nine

Saturday Morning: Leilani

"Rise and shine, chickadee."

The rusting springs of my crappy bed squawk as I sit bolt upright. My chest heaves, startled by the cheery words chirped in my ear. I whip my head around as my two besties cackle in witchy laughter—horrid crones.

"Dude, you were out cold," Bianca muses. She stands there in her standard black leggings, sports bra, and oversized flannel, arms crossed while she gazes down at me.

Melody stands beside her, wrapping an electrical cord around the hair dryer she swore she'd need but never ended up using.

"What time is it?" I ask, wiping the drool that's dried on my chin. Gross. But at least I feel rested. After a week of sleepless, squeaky nights, I must have finally gotten used to this horizontal torture device.

"Barely seven," Mel offers, returning to the floor beside her bunk to finish folding her clothes into perfectly formed piles.

Sweet, we have an hour and a half until breakfast.

Closing ceremonies directly follow.

Then it's time to go home.

I'm both ready and not ready to leave. At the end of camp in years past I felt a similar sensation, but this time it feels final. As though some cliché end of an era is upon me and nothing will ever be the same again. Ugh. I rub the sleep out of my eyes and flip back my blankets. The need to clear my muddled head overtakes all else.

"One last morning swim?" I hedge, sliding out of bed and snatching up my bikini. Even if they don't want to join, I'll go solo.

They look at each other and shrug.

"I'm in," Bee says.

"Same," Mel agrees, disrupting her neat piles in search of her suit.

A grin pulls at my lips, wide and unabashed. I'm lucky to be here with these two dynamo women. My heart is so full I barely notice the tiny breaks that had me aching last night. They'll heal.

With the love and support of my best friends, they'll heal.

ASIDE FROM THE usual mellow I feel at the end of every camp week, I'm in relatively high spirits. The dip in Heartbreak Lake did me some serious good. I'm refreshed and happily full after eating my bowl of oatmeal topped with cinnamon, brown sugar, and a fistful of trail mix for some added crunch—Mel is definitely on to something. I wash it all down with bitter black coffee that may or may not be reheated leftovers from yesterday morning.

All through breakfast I could feel Hudson's eyes on me. Charles had asked if we wanted to join the guys for breakfast, but before Bee or I could say anything, Mel charged in with a firm "no thanks" and then hurried us along like a mother duck corralling her ducklings. Neither Bianca nor I had the mental capabilities to sit with our ex-lovers, or ex-rival-turned-lover in my case. Melody could tell. She can always tell.

"How long are the closing ceremonies?" Mel asks as she bites into an orange slice. She hums blissfully as juice dribbles down her chin.

"About an hour. Give or take." I reach over with a napkin and dab at where the drops landed on her ample, exposed cleavage. "You've got quite the hoist going on this morning."

"Excuse me?" The peel falls from her fingers and lands right between her breasts, further proving my point.

"Looking to play bar wench with some lucky swashbuck-ler?" Bianca waggles her brows and aims a cashew at Mel's chest.

She swats it away before the nut can join the orange peel and tuts at us like we're being inappropriate. But the only thing vulgar here is the way her nipples are about to pop out of the top of her shirt.

"This is my last clean bra. I didn't realize I'd packed one a size too small," she assures us, though I'm not buying it. "Are they really that bad?"

"Bad?" Mel barks out a laugh. "Hell no, they're glorious."

"What she's trying to say is you look great," I soothe. "Better than great. You look sexy."

"I'm inclined to agree." A deep voice rumbles, startling all three of us. We crane our necks to see Everett standing beside our table, eyes set on Mel like she's a burger and he's a starving man who's been stranded on a deserted island for a decade. He clears his throat, seemingly pushing the lust aside. "Melody, may I borrow you for a moment?"

"Closing ceremonies are about to start," she says by way of rejection, but takes his outstretched hand anyway. His long fingers curl around hers.

"I'll happily take any time you're willing to give," he confesses breathlessly.

As Mel follows behind him, she throws an apologetic grin over her shoulder at us. "I'll be back soon. Don't leave without me."

"You drove," Bee responds, but Mel and Everett have already left the mess hall. Bianca sighs. "At least someone's getting some."

"Who are you trying to kid? I saw you tugging Kendrick into the bubbles last night." I snatch the last orange slice from Mel's abandoned plate and take a bite. "Do you honestly expect me to believe nothing happened?"

"Nothing happened," she deadpans.

"Bullshit."

"Really. I dragged him to the boathouse. We tried to fool around a bit, but I couldn't get a lady boner for the big guy. Talk about embarrassing. I told him I just wasn't into it, then left him half-undressed as I scurried out of there."

"You had Eddie on your mind?" I ask.

"What? No." Her quick defensiveness is cute. "Fine. Maybe a little. But not enough to start dating him."

"I feel that." I totally understand the urge to be with someone while also feeling like it's not right to go all in and date them. I'm still missing a piece when it comes to Hudson. I want to give things a try. It shouldn't seem like as big of a risk as it does, but . . . I can't help but be scared of what could go wrong. Or what could go right? I'm so messed up. Last night, after returning to our cabin, I stared at the ceiling for a couple of hours, trying to make heads or tails of my emotional smoothie, but to no avail.

"I don't think the guys are going to come back again next year," she tells me.

Nodding, I toss the orange peel onto my plate and stack it with hers and Mel's. She snatches our mugs and rises with me. We head to the garbage can to scrape our leftovers. "Hudson told me he definitely wasn't coming back."

"Is that because he's pretty sure you won the final capture the flag game? Is he already calling the bet?"

"No." I shake my head but provide nothing further. We wind through the noisy tables where campers are finishing up and soaking in the last moments of summer fun with their friends. So much carefree joy ripples through the room, that and a little B.O. from those who take the nostalgic week as permission to skimp on their personal hygiene routine. It's all so familiar and comforting that I'm feeling sad about going home.

"Mexico next year?" Bee asks, sensing my melancholy but also aiming to banish her own.

As much as it sucks knowing we won't be coming back to Evergreen Adventure Camp, I'm comforted with the absolution that my girls are by my side—if metaphorically, since Mel went off with a man.

"You know what?" I turn to my friend as we find a place in the field for the final camp gathering. "I think some piña coladas and cenotes sound perfect. Let's do Mexico next year."

Chapter Forty

Hudson

"Good morning, campers!" The screech of acoustic feedback wails as Astrid speaks into the microphone on stage. Beside her stands the hulking giant who owns this place, but he seems less imposing somehow. It might be the hint of a smile on his lips. Funny because I would have bet a lot of money that he didn't possess the muscles for that kind of facial expression. "I have a few announcements before we kick off the closing ceremonies. First, to whoever borrowed the blue mermaid tail last night, please return it to the docks before leaving the property. No questions asked. No one will get in trouble—"

"Shit," Charles mutters out of the side of his mouth, careful not to let Eddie hear. "I guess we forgot to put everything back."

"Where'd we take the fin off him?" I don't know about

Charles, but I was running on fumes last night when we mounted Eddie on the wall in the mess hall like a giant taxidermy bass. We giggled as he dangled there, passed out, mouth open, each of us taking turns posing next to him in full fisherman gear. I'm talking hat, pole, and vest with all those little lures dangling off the pockets. We managed to put the fishing stuff back in the boathouse, but for the life of me, I can't remember where we put that fin.

"Did we leave it down at the dock somewhere?" Charles muses.

"They probably would have found it by now if that were the case."

"Fair point."

"Did we even take it off of him?" At this point I'm not so sure. The end of the dwindling night is a blur in the light of day.

"No, you didn't." Charles and I startle and spin to face our friend who is wearing an amused grin. "I woke up at sunrise and thought for a moment that I'd turned into a merman. Until I realized it was probably another Weekend at Eddie's situation."

We all bust out laughing, three chuckleheads appreciating the longest-running prank of our friendship.

"Please tell me you got pictures," Eddie says, wiping away a tear.

"We tried to break into the office to find our phones, but our lock-picking skills are non-existent," I explain, intentionally omitting the part about running away when we heard sexy noises coming from inside.

"Aw, man."

"Don't worry," Charles reassures with an arm around Eddie's shoulder. "I found a vintage camera in the art room that had a few frames left on it. Everett's sure to get a surprise when he develops the film. I'll reach out in a day or two to ask for copies."

"I'm gonna miss this," I lament.

"Nah," Eddie shrugs. "We'll have fun wherever we go next year. New vacation, new mischief."

We all murmur our agreement and return our attention to the mess hall deck where Astrid is finishing up her announcements. It's almost time to announce the capture the flag winning team and the anticipation has my fingertips tingling. Not that it matters who won this year. I'm buzzed about being near Leilani one more time before we say goodbye.

"Would The Tidal Waves and Hudson Sucks please join me on stage?" Counselor Clark calls, wearing his signature sun protection starter kit, complete with wide-brimmed hat and zinc oxide stripe on his nose.

The crowd of campers parts as my teammates and I work our way through the throng and up the wooden steps. We stand to one side of Clark while Leilani and her team stand opposite us. I stare at the side of her face, willing her to look my way. Desperate for her to land her eyes on mine. She must feel my intensity because she turns and graces me with a subdued smile. It's all I can do to keep my feet planted instead of being lured to her like she's an angler and I'm hungry for worms.

Pussy-whipped isn't a strong enough term for how I feel.

I'm willing to do anything for her, all she'd have to do is ask and I wouldn't expect anything in return. Knowing I made her day a little bit brighter would be enough.

Which is why I'm about to make an ass of myself.

I unzip my hoodie in preparation as Clark taps on the microphone to ensure it's still working.

"It was a close game last night. All but two flags were found. One team found twenty-five, the other found twenty-six, meaning one *lowly* flag separates the victors from the losers."

Boy, this kid's got a flair for the dramatics. I wish he'd hurry up and announce who won. Not that it'll determine whether I follow through with my plan or not. I subtly toe off one of my shoes then the other. Fortunately, no one seems to notice. They're either too enthralled with the results or don't give a damn at all and are talking amongst themselves.

"The winner of this year's capture the flag tournament and the soon-to-be proud owner of the camp trophy for a year is," he pauses for effect. The irritated mumbles completely escape his notice.

I glimpse at Leilani, who's holding hands with her teammates, though something about her wince tells me Albert and Christina grabbed her hands rather than the other way around. She looks my way again and pulls a scowl of confusion as she spots my shoes sitting beside me.

"Can I get a drumroll?" the goofy counselor calls, and is instantly shot down by the crowd booing and yelling at him to "get on with it." He huffs a testy sigh. "Fine, fine. The winner is Hudson Sucks!"

Leilani and her teammates cheer and high-five each other and then step toward Clark to accept the beat-up trophy that's four feet tall and clearly meant for a golf tournament. There's a tiny orange triangle taped to the end of the club that's mid-backswing over the golfer's shoulder. Kendrick, being the tallest of the group, holds the award over his head and the team leads the crowd in a rousing chant of *Hudson Sucks*.

Which is when I make my move.

I drop my hoodie to the ground and Clark gives a little yelp as I snatch the mic from his hands.

"Can I have everyone's attention?" I say a little too loudly, forgetting for a second that my voice is amplified and there's no need to shout. The crowd quiets, and I'm surprised as Astrid braces an arm out to stop Clark from retrieving the microphone from me. Instead, she grins and nods my way, even though there's no way she knows what I'm about to do.

"This is my fifth and final year here at camp and I just want to say that each year has been better than the last. This woman"—I gesture to Leilani, whose eyes are wide and unblinking—"is the reason I've had so much fun. The rivalry I share with Leilani Walker lights up my soul, whether I'm here or holed up in my office wishing I were here. She challenges me to be my best in all the ways that count, and that's gradually extended to life outside of camp as well."

She steps forward, places a hand over the mic. "Hudson, what the fuck are you doing?"

"Making a spectacle," I murmur in her ear, noting the sweet tangerine scent of her, before putting the microphone back to my lips and continuing on. "Every year, we make a bet about what the winner gets, and each year, the stakes of the bet have increased. But this year, I made the decision to call it off, and while Leilani may think it's unfair that I made the call for both of us—especially since her team won—I'm offering a consolation prize to make it up to her."

I hand her the microphone and proceed to remove my shirt. A few campers whistle from the crowd while others laugh, clearly reading the words *Hudson Sucks* written all over my chest and arms. I quickly unbutton and shuck my pants. As I tuck my thumbs into the waistband of my boxer briefs, I lock eyes with Leilani.

"I'll never forget our summers together; least of all this one," I say, then hastily drop my undies before I lose the nerve. "And I hope to see you around town someday."

Before she can respond, I cup my junk, leap off the deck and streak across the open field. Cheers and hollers and gasps follow me as I bolt through the campers and dart toward the tree line.

This may very well be the last time I see Leilani Walker, but I know for damned sure that the image of *Hudson Sucks* hand-painted across my ass cheeks will stick with her for years to come.

Chapter Forty-One

Leilani

"Would you look at that. It's a full moon this morning," I hear Astrid say with a chuckle even as Russell tries to cover her eyes.

What the hell just happened?

I mean, I know what happened, but I still find myself gawking as Hudson scurries into the trees, covered in my team's name.

Astrid sidles up to me, still giggling. "That's one way to leave a lasting impression."

"And then some," I mutter.

She nudges me with her shoulder. A familiar waft of pine and cedar fills my nostrils, but as I glance around, I see that Russell is still farther back on the stage. The scent is coming from Astrid.

"You smell nice," I say suggestively.

Her cheeks pop red even as she shrugs and looks over her shoulder. "I'm wearing something new these days."

"I bet you are." I like this for her. She seems smilier than usual—if that's even possible—and someone that smells an awful lot like a forest appears to be the cause.

"Are you going after him?" Astrid nods toward the tree line.

"Haven't decided. Can I ask you a question?"

She nods. "Of course."

"There's no way of knowing which flags we did and didn't find from last night's game, is there?"

"Not usually, no."

I deflate a little until I realize she said "usually."

"But this year?" I press.

She rolls her eyes and throws a thumb over her shoulder at Russell. "Tightwad over here wanted to make sure we get every single one back so we're not 'spending unnecessary funds' on buying more for next week's group. He had us number each flag and make a spreadsheet so we could find the ones left out there."

"Which flags weren't found?" Regardless of how much I try to convince myself it doesn't matter, I have to know what Hudson did with the flag he found when we hooked up.

She fumbles through the pages on her clipboard and finds the correct one. After skimming her finger down the rows of numbers, she says, "Here we are. Looks like you guys missed the one at the top of the wall on the obstacle course and the one in the pump house."

"And you're sure?"

"Yep." She nods, flips the pages back in place, and reaches out for the microphone I'm still holding. "I'd better get things back on track."

"Thanks, Astrid," I murmur, handing it over.

She addresses the crowd, apologizing for the interruption, and launches into more announcements. She mentions something about everyone visiting the Art Barn to check out the showcase, but I'm not paying any attention.

I'm still focused on Hudson's spectacle.

It's a bad idea.

I know it is even as I hop off the stage in pursuit of the butt cheek bandit who streaked across camp in a blaze of nude glory.

I trot in the direction Hudson went, unsure if I'll find him hiding among the trees full of regret, or if he's high-tailing it to his cabin to cover up.

"Leilani," Bianca hollers, breaking through my haze.

My feet pause only long enough to toss her a quick, "I need to go—"

"I know," she insists with a cheeky grin, and before I can do or say anything, she pulls me into a hug. A surprisingly gropey hug where her hands are all over my butt and deep in my back pocket. She finally lets me go with a little smack on my ass cheek.

"What the hell?"

Bee winks. "Just in case. You can thank me later."

I can't even unpack how weird my friend is because I'm too busy jogging into the woods to search the paths. No luck, so I pivot and head toward Hudson's cabin. As I pass the men's shower, I pause because I swear there's water running in there. And since camp is pretty much over, there shouldn't be anyone in the building.

What am I doing?

I shove out rational thought as my sneakers squelch in the puddles of water dotting the concrete. Nearing the only shower running, I hear a masculine voice mumbling incoherently. It's Hudson. It has to be. That or I'm about to embarrass some poor sap who thought he could get a quick, private shower in while everyone else is at closing ceremonies.

Without stopping to consider . . . well, anything . . . I pull back the curtain and catch the full view of a muscular back, legs, and the most biteable ass I've ever seen. What's more, *Hudson Sucks* is scrawled all over every inch in different sizes and colors.

He must have heard me coming because he doesn't even flinch at my intrusion; he just keeps on facing away under the sad trickle of water.

"Figured I might find you here," I say, while trying my best to swallow my lust.

"You're quite the detective," he deadpans, and for a moment, I consider whether this was a mistake, but I can't convince myself to leave.

"What do I win for cracking the case?" I ask, then snort because I said crack and his plump ass is on full display. I'm feeling all kinds of awkward, which is new for me. Normally, I'm so self-assured, but right now? My attempt at playing it cool is failing miserably.

"What do you want?" he asks huskily.

"That all depends."

"On?"

"Did you finish my team's banner after we left the Art Barn on Tuesday?" I hadn't let myself truly consider that he'd done it until seeing the same words all over his body. The Hudson Pratt I'm used to would never disparage or make fun of himself. Even if it was all in good fun. Yet here he stands, naked in the shower covered in a team name that directly mocks him.

Winds of change? A small one, perhaps. But enough small changes add up to real growth, and I'm suddenly obsessed with the idea that maybe this man has, in fact, changed.

"Did you?" I ask again.

"I did."

"What about the anonymous donations to my teen center?" Even as I say it I know it's a reach. If I would have won last year he would have been on the hooks for fifty bucks each month for the rest of his life. Five-hundred each month is a considerably larger gift.

But he surprises me by nodding while still refusing to face me.

I'm speechless for a moment. My heart thrums wildly in my chest, the accelerated cadence heating my neck and tingling my scalp.

"And the flag in the pump house?" I hedge, because it'd be yet another tick in the column of change. "What did you do with it?"

"I threw it away."

"Why?"

"Because I don't want to win you anymore." His voice is hoarse, ravaged like he's trying to keep it together.

I instantly deflate.

Should it hurt my feelings that he stopped wanting to win that date with me? Whether it should or shouldn't, it stings. It makes me feel sadder than I'd ever admit to anyone. I cross my arms over my chest to quell the dull ache taking root. "Why not? What changed?"

"I'd much rather *deserve* you, Leilani." Hudson finally turns and faces me. "And even more than that, I want you to want me too."

There's a desperate vulnerability in his eyes. Lines at the corners that give away the weight of what he's putting out there.

Something clicks in me as I accept that I want the same thing.

Any lingering animosity drifts up and away like the mist floating around the shower stall. This rivalry, in the form we've held onto for years, no longer suits me and I'm encouraged that he feels the same. I'm pretty sure Hudson Pratt will still manage to push my buttons, but maybe that doesn't have to be a bad thing.

"Then let me be forward and say that I do want you." I shift toward him and stop as he holds up a hand.

"For clarity's sake," he says, forehead still scrunched. "Are you willing to go out with me? On a date? Because you *want* to? Or do you only want something physical here and now?"

I uncross my arms and slide my fingers between his,

pressing our palms together. He responds to my squeeze with one of his own. The corner of his lips tick up, and his breathing speeds.

"Can't we do both?" I ask.

"Yes. Absolutely." Joy and relief spread over his face as his lips break into a wide smile. He's practically glowing as water condenses and drips from his temple, the tip of his nose, from his chin onto that bare chest of his. My eyes feast on the sexy spectacle of his nude, wet, chiseled body. Words scribbled all over. Drops of water trail down his chest, dragging various colors in streaks over rippling abs. I want to follow every drip down his body. He's sexy as hell, and it has my knees quaking.

And when I finally focus on his large, already hard erection, I burst out laughing. Because along its length are the words Property of Leilani Walker.

"Are you laughing at my cock, Leilani?" His voice is low, scolding, and it sends a shiver speeding up my spine.

"What if I am?" I ask, popping out my hip and settling my hand on top.

He watches my movements, hungry and hopeful. "Then I think you should say sorry and make it up to me."

Chapter Forty-Two

Hudson

Leilani Walker wants to date me.

I am so freaking full of excitement over the prospect that I consider hauling her to my car to take her out right now.

Until she refocuses my attention by stepping forward to close the gap between us. My muscles flex under her touch as she settles a hand on my shoulder. She leans in, pressing up on her tiptoes.

"I'm sorry, Hudson." Her breathy apology puffs on the shell of my ear and it makes me groan low in antsy frustration. But when her teeth catch my earlobe in a gentle nibble, all bets are off.

I encircle her waist and spin her so she's under the shower with me. Caged in between my arms and the wall. Her gasp is cute, and it ignites a consuming heat in my chest.

Leaving this stall is the furthest thing from my mind. Not before I've had my fill. But the notion that I will ever get enough of this woman makes me want to laugh.

There is no reality in which I will ever have my fill of Leilani Walker.

"I accept your apology," I say, huffing out something between a laugh and a moan.

"I'm not done apologizing," she says, sliding her hand down my chest, toying along my abs until she grabs hold of my aching cock. Pleasure sizzles through my veins as she glides her skilled fingers from my base up to the head and back down again. She is in control, and it's driving me mad in all the best ways. I tear my gaze from her eyes and look down to where she strokes the sloppily applied words off of my length. She smears my handiwork until nothing remains besides clean skin.

"Perfect," she says and sinks to her knees.

She is a vision. A soaking wet goddess kneeling before me, licking her lips like I'm some treat she's been craving. She still has a firm hold on the base of my cock and a lock on my eyes. I watch, not daring to breathe for fear that this is a dream and the slightest stutter will rip me from my fantasy.

But while this *is* a dream, it's also real. Nothing proves it like feeling the tip of her tongue dragging along the underside of my shaft. Her licks and kisses are gentle and whisper light. The barely there touch weakens my knees. I'm shaking at the sight of her, the feel of her. But I tense as her full lips find my tip and slip lazily down, just past the head. With the same speed, she recedes, then takes more of me with the next dip.

"You're killing me, Walker." My hips twitch as I desperately keep from thrusting farther into her mouth. She's taking the lead, I love it, but it's so damn hard to maintain my sanity.

And she fucking knows it too.

I feel her chuckle as she descends even more. She's playing with me like I'm a toy here for her amusement. My heart races against my rib cage, erratic thumps that should be alarming, only I'm not worried or scared because I'd happily die right here on the spot if this is the way I go. Getting sucked by the woman responsible for all my lust-fueled fantasies over the last four years.

Of its own accord, my hand slides into her hair and grips. But before I can tell it to loosen and apologize, she hums in encouragement and reaches for my other wrist. She presses it to her scalp and on reflex, I grip there too.

"Do you want me to take over?" I ask, the words croaking low in my throat.

She nods and releases her grip on the base of me.

I test gently at first. Pulling back to where I almost slip out of her mouth, before sliding back in, but farther than she had me before. Back out, then gently in. My clumsy hold on control deteriorates as I increase the speed of each thrust. Before I realize it, my legs are tight and I'm fucking deep into her hot little mouth. She spurs me on, moaning and sloppy as she takes my cock. I push until I nudge the back of her throat. She's taking nearly all of me, and if her noises and unwavering eye contact are any indicators, she's loving it just as much as I am.

"If I knew how fucking good . . . I would have slid into your bratty little mouth and fucked the snark right out of it. You're taking me so deep. So good. So *fucking* good."

My low back begins to tighten, and I can tell I'm about to come. While I want that eventually, there are other things I need to do first. With any other woman, the old me would have enjoyed the blow job, said "thanks, babe," and been on his way.

Not the new me.

And *not* with Leilani Walker.

I press once more, deeper than ever, and pull out as she coughs. Mascara is smeared under her spiky lashes. I pull her up to me. I gently drag my thumb over her lips, which are swollen from my onslaught. Picturing where they were a moment ago sends vibrations through my limbs.

"Now you're allowed to accept my apology." She nips at my thumb then grins.

Laughter rumbles up my chest. "What was that for again?"

"Fuck if I know," she chuckles. "But you can still accept it."

"What if instead of saying I accept it, I show you that I accept it?" I offer as I press my fingertips into her sides and nibble on her ear.

"This is all becoming so convoluted," she says with an antsy little sigh.

"What do you suggest instead?" I ask, still playing along,

though I'd agree. All I'm capable of focusing on is this woman and the way her denim shorts are pressed against my erection.

The groan that leaves my lips as she slides her hand down between us and grabs my sensitive cock bounces off the walls of the men's showers.

Her other hand digs into one of the pockets of those little shorts of hers. My blurry eyes come into sharp focus as she holds up a little foil packet and says, "I say we finish what I started."

Chapter Forty-Three

Leilani

The way Hudson's pupils dilate even more is astounding; there's barely any iris left. And his erection is impossibly hard in my grip. I'm anxious to have him inside of me again. Last night feels too far away.

He eyes the condom I'm holding between my pointer and middle fingers.

"Where'd you get that?" he asks, sucking on my neck just above the dip in my collarbone.

"It's Bianca's. Or was Bianca's." I'm struggling to focus as Hudson shoves his hands beneath my shirt to toy with my nipples. He flicks and pinches and I'm right on the edge of agony. "Sh-she stopped me and shoved it in my pocket."

Suddenly, Hudson is pulling my tank top up over my head. He struggles a bit with the built-in bra part but finally succeeds and tosses the complicated garment to the wet tiles with a growl. He crouches and nuzzles my breast before sucking a stiff peak between his lips. His teeth nibble and drag and I can't keep my hips from pressing toward him.

"Remind me to send your friend a fruit basket," he purrs while smothering my other nipple with the same attention.

"She'd probably rather have replacements."

"A safe-sex basket, then." Hudson holds tightly to my hips and trails kisses down my belly, stopping to appreciate the piercing I got a few months ago. "When the hell did you get this, Walker?"

"In M-May," I stutter. He's unbuttoning my shorts and it's so hard to concentrate. "For my birthday."

"Taurus, hmm?" The zipper comes down slowly until my shorts flop open.

"Yes," I gasp while he plays with the sopping wet strings at the bottom of my shorts and slides a few fingers under the fabric to explore.

"Should have known."

"Why?" I'm quaking. My knees would be knocking if he didn't have them spread so wide.

"Because of what a stubborn little brat you are." His voice rumbles against my hip bone, calling attention to how close he is to my core. I want to clap back, but I'm too busy. Too distracted with his attention.

One solid tug and my shorts are a puddle at my feet. I'm left with nothing but a skimpy pair of black cheekies with pink hearts all over them. He drags a finger along the edge of the fabric.

"Cute," he mutters, "but they gotta go."

Hudson peels off my panties. They're soaking wet from the shower, sure, but there's no doubt that how much he's turned me on is a contributing factor too. He helps me step out of my shorts and undies, but when I lift a knee to reach for the laces on my shoes, he grabs my wrist.

"You're going to leave those on," he demands, looking up and holding my stare.

"Really?"

"Oh yeah."

"You have a thing for banging a woman wearing nothing but sneakers?" My chuckle fades quickly as he grazes a knuckle up my thigh and along my dripping seam.

"I have a thing for *you* in only sneakers," he murmurs, pressing a finger deep into me, then curls it to hit the perfect angle. I bite my lip to keep from screaming. "Ever since the panty raid, when you came chasing after me to give me the lacy, blue thong. Your sneakers were untied. It's like you were so worried I'd be gone if you took the time to tie them."

He pumps in and out of me, picking up speed. The sound is wet and vulgar. If anyone were to walk in, they'd know exactly what he was doing to me.

"That's a pretty . . . oh . . . flimsy theory," I'm barely able to utter. A moan pushes through my lips, elbowing any other attempted words out of the way.

"I ate up any hint that you might've wanted me." His breath is hot against my pussy. And then it's his tongue searing against my throbbing clit. It's almost too much to handle: him finger fucking me while he laps at the spot that aches and aches and has me writhing with pleasure.

The cliff is fast approaching and I am anxious to leap over the edge.

"I'm close," I whimper then grumble with frustration as he pulls his lips and tongue away.

"Say it again but with my name," he demands, keeping up the rhythm of his manual onslaught.

I scowl down at him—who's being the brat now?

He grins and dips his tongue back in for a single swirl. I'm a mere skip away from orgasm, but he's holding me at enough of a distance that there's no hope of coming unless he gives me just a little bit more. "Say it."

I grip fistfuls of his hair and practically growl, "I'm close, Hudson."

"That's my good girl," he chuckles.

But before I can get on him about praise not being my kink, he's sucking hard on my clit and fingering the fuck out of me and I'm careening over the edge. I tumble and shudder and scream, all the while Hudson calling me a good girl loops in my mind. And I realize I don't hate it, especially if it leads to coming this hard.

I don't have time to rebound because Hudson stands and snatches my wrists. He tugs them up toward the showerhead.

"Hold on," he barks, pressing my fingers around the pipe between the showerhead and the wall.

I do as he says and am rewarded with a mind-numbing kiss. His tongue dives deeply into my mouth, and I can taste the pleasure he gave me. The pleasure that's still wracking my body, clenching my core.

The foil packet rips and he's rolling the condom over his dick and I'm fidgeting in anticipation.

"Legs around my waist, Walker." His fingers press divots into my thighs as he helps me hop up where he wants me.

Hudson holds me in place, despite my desperate wiggling. I want him to lower me already, but all he's doing is slipping my wet slit all over the head of his cock.

"Do you want me, Leilani?" His words are level. How is he so calm? I'm over here losing my mind, physically begging him to rail me, and he's asking me goddamned questions.

"I want you," I whimper then rejoice as he slowly lowers me down only to stop as the head of his cock slips inside. Then he pauses and I wriggle for more.

"Do you want to date me?"

No doubt my eyes flash and fling daggers at his, but all he can manage is a cheeky grin, brown hair flopping over his brow in that mischievous way I'm beginning to crave.

I nod. "I want to date you, Hudson."

His eyes roll back in bliss, and he utters some kind of appreciation to the ceiling.

I'm about to giggle because there's no way going out with me should make him this happy, but the laugh catches in my throat and turns into a mewling wail of pleasure as he slips me down the rest of the way. I'm seated on his cock, stretching to accommodate his size and shaking from the pressure and remnants of my orgasm.

He groans around a chuckle, as if he can't believe how good I feel pulled taut around him. His facial expressions are fascinating. I can't help but watch him as bliss and joy and hunger morph his handsome features. All of his emotions play out like a movie and I'm left wondering if the same thing was happening in the pump house when he had me bent over. I couldn't see him, only felt and relished the naughty things he did to me. I'm suddenly anxious for more of this to see if each time affects him so strongly.

But then all thoughts drop away as he hoists my ass and starts plunging into my needy pussy with wild abandon. His forehead tilts to rest against mine. Eyes oscillating from my face down to where we connect and back again like he can't decide what's a more delicious sight.

"Oh fuck, Hudson."

"Yeah?" He's nodding jerkily, movements matching his erratic thrusts.

"Yes," I whimper.

Release is fast approaching for both of us. My head swims with it.

"Me too, Walker."

He pants and squeezes my ass cheeks for one final thrust then holds me tight to his body. The groan that leaves his lips is so satisfied, so similar to how I feel that my heart swoops low in my belly. I'm shuddering. He's shuddering. His heart rages against his rib cage, and I'm suddenly a little concerned if he's ok.

"Hudson?" I ask, releasing the shower pipe and placing a hand over his sternum. We lock eyes and he smiles.

"My heart's fine." He leans in for a little kiss, nibbling my lip like he's tasting me.

"I just wanted to make sure." Thoughts of his heart

attack flood my mind, and I'm suddenly wondering if this is good for his health. I'm finally starting to like the guy; I'd hate to be the reason he lands back in the hospital.

He clasps a hand over mine, lifts it to his lips, then returns it to his chest.

"It's finally beating the way it should."

He's being cheesy, and it makes me roll my eyes.

I'd be lying if I said I didn't like it.

But I won't be confessing that to him anytime soon.

Chapter Forty-Four

Hudson

"I suddenly regret my choices," Leilani gripes as she wrestles with her wet tank top. She's struggling to pull it down over her breasts. The clingy fabric sticks to itself and catches on her damp skin.

"I'm not." I offer, enjoying the view immensely. Any extra moment I get to check out her glorious, naked body is a moment to cherish. But the more she wriggles, the more I want to rip her shirt back off and shove her against the shower stall. Which would be all well and good, except check out is in forty-five minutes, and I don't have a single article of clothing to cover my equipment.

Leilani turns and scowls at me. She pauses her efforts, tank top pulled down over one tit and wedged in the opposite armpit—she looks close to admitting defeat.

"So, you don't want me to get clothes from your cabin?

Because I'd be happy to finish dressing and waltz on out of here so you can fend for yourself." She gestures to my dick that's been gradually stiffening since she started squirming around in front of me. "I'm sure Astrid and Russell would be totally cool with you continuing to run around, hanging brain all over camp."

She has a point.

I snatch her by the wrist and pull her up against me. The hiss I make from connecting with her cold, wet shirt makes her laugh. I settle my lips on hers, swallowing her giggle. She presses up against me and, oh, look at that. My semi has upgraded to a full-on erection.

Best if I get this under control before it's too late.

"Want some help?" I offer, wishing we could stay naked all day instead.

"Yeah, if you could get this band down past my boob—"

She shifts so I can grip the elastic band and pull it out from beneath her arm. With her help, it settles around her rib cage, securing her breasts in place. She pulls the rest of her shirt down with a satisfied sigh. "I guess we've answered the age-old questions of how many brunettes it takes to put on a wet, built-in bra tank top."

I snort.

She smiles at me and my heart melts. This woman. How wonderful it is to be on the receiving end of her happiness. I'd say I feel content, but my boner's making me a little antsy. Leilani bends over to pick up her wet undies and I advance on her. She moans as I slip my knuckles along her sex, still slick from fucking. Her knees press together, her back arches, and I take that as an invitation to press inside and curl my fingers.

"Hudson."

I love my name on her tongue, but this one is tinted with caution.

She's right. We have shit to do.

Reluctantly, I pull back and leave her with a little slap on the ass. She yelps and stands bolt upright. She squawks even more when I snatch the wet panties from her hands.

"Hudson," she warns, brows lowered, hands on her hips.

"I'm keeping them."

"Between these"—she points to the pair I'm holding—"the ones you ripped in the pump house, and your hump day panty flag, I'm running pretty low on underwear. Keep this up and I won't have any left."

"Oops. You stumbled on my master plan." My over-the-top villain laugh cuts off as she cracks her palm over my bare butt cheek. "Ouch! You've got slappy little hands. Now I'm keeping this pair out of spite."

"Fine. Keep it," she huffs. The wet denim shorts she picks up slide on easier than her shirt did, but she gives a little shiver once they're in place. I can only imagine how the cold material feels against her hot, aching pussy— "Eyes up here, Pratt. Focus."

"Right. Right."

"I'll be back in a couple minutes." She eeks around me and pushes the shower curtain aside.

"You remember which bunk bed is mine?" I ask as she scurries toward the door in bow-legged strides. It looks like she's been riding a horse for hours. The proud grin that spreads across my face gives me away.

"I'm walking like this because of the wet clothes," she chastises.

"Tell yourself whatever you like," I purr, crossing my arms and leaning against the stall wall. I have half a mind to grab her and actually fuck her until she walks funny, but I'm still naked and precious time is running out.

Time be damned because she saunters back over, and for a moment, I think she might be down for another session, especially when she lays her hands on my pecs and leans in for a slow, sultry kiss. God, her mouth. She tastes so sweet, and I lose myself a little as her tongue sweeps against mine. But it's over all too soon, and I groan as she retreats.

"See you later," she says, and makes her way to the exit. I watch her go, dazed and drunk on her affections. But something niggles at the back of my mind.

Her wording.

See you later.

Doesn't exactly sound like something someone would say if they were coming back in a couple minutes.

"*Walker,*" I warn, stepping out of the stall and toward her. She backs away quickly, just out of my reach, until she's out of the building and standing in the sunlight.

"Bye, Pratt." She blows me a kiss and jogs down the path toward the parking lot.

Which also happens to be in the opposite direction from my cabin.

"Are you still going to go out with me?" I call. I'm pretty

sure I know the answer, but a twinge of doubt weasels its way in as I watch her receding form.

She pauses and spins around, wearing a mirthful smile. "Of course."

In an instant, she's gone, but I'm still alight with joy. If one final camp prank is what she needs, who am I to deny her?

But the whole me being naked thing is still a problem. I scour the showers for a pair of left-behind shorts or a towel. Hell, I'd settle for a washcloth at this point. After a quick scan, I come up empty-handed. The only things in here are the mildewy plastic shower curtains—you couldn't pay me enough—and the cheeky little panties Leilani left behind.

Chapter Forty-Five

Leilani

"So? How did it go?" Bianca asks, scrutinizing my wet clothes. She waggles her eyebrows in a way that suggests she already has a pretty solid idea of how things went.

"See for yourself," I say, tugging her to the edge of the parking lot where there's an obstructed view of the men's shower. Through the trees, we can see Hudson peek out. He must think the coast is clear because he exits the building and scurries toward his cabin. "Damn. I thought he'd be naked."

"What's he wearing?" Bee can't hide her chuckle.

I can't either because the sight of him squeezed into my undies has me belly laughing. Especially since every few steps he has to dig them out of his crack because they are way too small.

"My panties," I explain through bouts of laughter.

My friend high-fives me and calls toward a retreating—nearly nude—Hudson, "Nice cheeks, cowboy!"

He trips a little and comes to a stop. But even at this distance, I can see his gleaming grin as he flips us the bird.

The two of us whistle at him, hollering vulgar comments that should make him blush, but it only makes him walk more slowly, strutting with each step. Eventually, he disappears into the trees.

"What are we yelling at?"

Bianca and I turn to find a beaming Melody, dragging her rolling luggage behind.

"Leilani fucked Hudson in the shower—"

"I never said that," I interrupt.

"—then left him with only her panties to wear back to his cabin."

Mel turns to me. "Really?"

Denying it is useless. "That's how it went down. And we're going to go out next weekend."

"What? That's great!"

"Thanks, Mom," I snark, then yelp as she hauls off and smacks my ass.

"One for the road," she explains, then rolls her bag toward her car. She pops the trunk and we all huck our luggage inside. "Put a towel down before you get in so you don't get my seats wet."

"I call shotgun," I blurt, which is immediately followed by Bianca's groan. But she crawls into the back seat and buckles up in the middle without further complaint. After I've laid out my beach towel and settled into the passenger seat, I turn to Mel. "Are you glad you came with us to camp?"

"Definitely," she says, and I'd have to be blind to miss the way her cheeks turn a telling shade of pink. The mascara smudges under her eyes and speckles of paint in her hair don't escape my notice either.

Part of me wants to ask, but the rest of me knows Mel will be tight-lipped about whatever happened this week until she's ready to share. If nothing else, the grin on her face says it all.

We drive down the lumpy gravel road that leads to Highway 101. I watch the old wooden Evergreen Adventure Camp sign fade out the back window as Melody speeds toward home. The familiar glum of leaving camp yet again fills my chest, momentarily intensified as I realize I won't ever be coming back. Some of my best (and craziest) memories were made there—solid bonds with new friends forged among the towering trees and crackling campfire. It's sad to say goodbye, but a lightness takes over the melancholy as I think about the connection I made with my rival.

Former rival.

I'm looking forward to going on a date with Hudson Pratt—words I'd never thought before—and hopefully this sexy little tryst will morph into something worthwhile.

I grin cheekily out the window.

And maybe, just maybe, this isn't officially our last week of camp.

Epilogue

Four Months Later: Hudson

The suit feels weird. So do the polished shoes that have been living in the back of my closet for nearly a year. The lavender tie is tight around my neck, and I'm suddenly wondering how I wore these constricting outfits for so many years without being miserable.

Except, I was miserable then.

But not anymore.

Despite the uncomfortable getup, I'm bright and effervescent inside. Practically bounding up the stairs to the third-floor condo with flowers in hand and a whistle on my tongue. I'd wear anything for her. And since this is our first date, the suit is a must.

Woah, woah. I know what you're thinking.

But Hudson, why did you wait four months to *finally* take Leilani out on a date?

I tried!

The weekend after we came back, we planned to meet at a coffee shop down on Ruston and walk along the waterfront. But the second I handed her a latte, she asked if I wanted to go back to her place. And I'm no idiot, so of course I agreed.

Since then, we have spent a ton of time together. Pizza and movies on the couch. Walks around Pt. Defiance. She even made me go to her CrossFit gym and let me tell you . . . I thought I was in great shape, but by the end I was wishing for another heart attack just to get out of the next set of burpees.

And we've tried to go out on more formal dates. Honest. I had tickets to a concert and dinner reservations at this awesome Thai restaurant nearby, but the second I saw her in her cutoff shorts and vintage band T-shirt, our plans changed. To make it up to her, I put on a special, one-night-only performance in her bedroom that evening. I'm not a karaoke guy, but I gave it my damndest to help her realize she was better off missing the Weezer concert. There are countless other similar examples.

But this time . . .

This time we are going on a date if it's the last thing I do. My girlfriend deserves to be wined and dined.

I've also decided I'm going to tell her I love her for the first time. Don't get me wrong, I didn't just fall in love with Leilani Walker recently. A part of me has been in love with her for multiple years. But I've finally worked up the nerve to come out with it.

Plus, one of my high-rolling clients helped me get access

to the chef's table in the new upscale gastro pub that opened last month.

Again, I feel you worrying that I returned to a douchey life of being an insufferable business-bro. Let me save you the antacids and tell you I didn't. I started my own social media marketing business, one that's geared toward helping small companies and non-profits in the greater Tacoma area. To help supplement those operations that don't have deep pockets, I've taken on a handful of what I like to call "benefactor businesses" that pay a premium with the understanding that the elevated fee goes toward discounting rates for other clients who need a hand up. They get good publicity and tax write-offs while I get to continue serving businesses that can really use my expertise.

We launched two months ago, and so far, so good. Time will tell how sustainable it all is, but in the meantime, my work has filled something in my soul I didn't know was missing. I feel like I'm finally doing what I'm meant to do, with so much less stress on my heart than my old shitty, demanding job.

All in all, your guy's doing really well.

Great job.

Incredible girlfriend.

And about to go on a fancy date with said incredible girlfriend.

Life couldn't get better.

I reach Leilani's door and ring the bell, a huge bouquet of sunflowers clenched in my fist. It's weird, but I'm a little nervous. My heart thuds against my chest, rapping out a rhythm that doesn't line up with a normal pulse.

But all those nerves drop away as she opens the door.

My mouth falls open and the flowers dangle at my side as I take in Leilani, who's wearing a form-fitting emerald green dress. Her thick, shiny hair is pulled into a sexy twist at the back of her head. I can practically envision pulling the picks that hold the complicated style in place so that her heavy waves fall all over her bare shoulders. My eyes roam all over her, drinking in the most gorgeous woman in the world.

"I'm almost ready," she says, leaning in for a quick peck then disappearing into a condo I've become very familiar with. She continues talking even as I walk into the kitchen and pull the cellophane off the bouquet I brought. "Shoes, earrings, and lip gloss, and we'll be off. Thank you for the flowers. They're beautiful."

"You're welcome. And take your time," I call to her, while snipping the ends of the sunflowers and arranging them in a vase I found on top of a cabinet. I add water, place it on the counter, and stroll down the hall to Leilani's room where she's tossing shoes out of her closet. She's on her hands and knees, digging through a pile of footwear, mumbling all the swear words.

That naughty mouth of hers.

"Want a hand?" I ask, trying ever so hard to focus on offering help instead of picturing her naked and in the same position.

"Yeah." She settles back on her haunches and brushes an

errant strand of hair off her face. "I bought a new pair the other day. I don't think they even made it out of the box."

I glance around her room, which is usually quite tidy. But today, there are dresses, shoes, and—gulp—lacy lingerie strewn about. If these are the cast-offs, what is she wearing under that silky green fabric? My mind and pulse go crazy picturing what I'll be finding when I unwrap her later tonight.

I shake my head and dig around the piles on her bed. No luck. Then I'm on to the floor, where I lift a couple of towels and bingo.

"Found 'em."

"Thank fuck," she says with a relieved sigh. Her smile drops as she reaches for the box and I pull them out of reach. "Hudson."

"Allow me," I say, gently pressing on her shoulder so she sits on the edge of the bed. I kneel before her and set the shoes to the side. My eyes are on hers and I bask in the affectionate, cheeky smirk she's wearing.

With gentle care, I encircle one of her ankles and bring it up to rest on my chest. She wiggles her toes a little, and I take in the gold polish glittering in the low light of her side table lamps. Her breath hitches as I glide my fingers up her shin to press the slick green fabric up her thigh. I don't miss the way her hips fidget like she wants me to touch her higher.

But I'm trying to be well-behaved.

Still not breaking eye contact, I snatch one of her strappy gold shoes and fit it onto her foot. After securing the delicate buckle, I graze my lips over her skin, then tend to her other foot in the same way.

I'm pretty sure I spot a flash of disappointment when the other heel is in place, and that simply won't do.

"What are you doing?" Leilani asks breathlessly as I slide her ankles over my shoulders.

"Do you even have to ask?"

"Aren't we going to miss our reservation?" She's saying the words even as she's leaning back against the pile of her rejected formal wear.

"Maybe." I duck my head under her dress. Her knees press wide to accommodate my shoulders and allow me the unfiltered access I never seem to stop craving.

"Do we have enough time?" She's writhing, I haven't even touched her where she's hot and wet, and already that hitch in her voice and wiggle of her hips is giving her away.

I chuckle as she digs her heels into my back, pulling me closer until I'm a breath away from her sexy little pussy.

"For a taste of you, Leilani Walker? Always."

The End

Camp Clandestine Book 2
Hearts and Crafts

Melody

Half an hour later, our water bottles are filled and activities are selected. Both Leilani and I signed up for morning swim—we even snuck Bianca's name in with ours in case she doesn't make it out here in time. That way if she has the opportunity to join us she's already on the list.

I left my afternoons open so I could nap or read or follow whatever flight of fancy I might have after a full morning. Leave a little room for spontaneity for once in my life instead of scheduling myself until I drop. And for whatever reason the intentional "scheduling" of free time leaves me with an almost giddy feeling, like I'm getting off on a lack of structure instead of letting it incite the usual panic.

Who am I?

But what I'm most excited for is arts and crafts after lunch. I'm not exactly sure what that will entail but whether it's painting, or sculpting, or hell, even making candles, I don't care.

Before I became a mom—then doubled down and became a working mom—my life was filled with all manner of the arts. I took every creative class I was qualified for in high school and that extended to college. Back then, I had my favorites mediums, but I've been so far removed from that world that I don't even know what I *like* anymore. This week will probably do little more than dust the cobwebs off my creative mind. But regardless, it'll be great to dip my toes back into the water, so to speak.

"I need to run to the bathroom," Leilani mentions. "Did you want to come?"

"Nah, I think you can manage on your own," I tease and yelp when she presses her cold water bottle to the back of my neck in retribution. I haul back and give her a solid whack on her back pocket. She narrows her gaze, but lets a smile loose as she turns to head for the restrooms.

We plan to meet later at the opening ceremonies on the main lawn and just like that I'm left to my own devices. Instinctively, I reach for my phone only to remember we turned those in at check-in. The no-cell-phone policy is wild to me and really shines a light on how much time I waste scrolling through whatever garbage is available.

With time on my hands, I stroll past one of the information tables and snag a map of the grounds. Maybe I'll swing by the Art Barn for a peak at the studio where we'll be doing arts and crafts. I locate and follow the correct trail and quickly find myself breaking through a thick line of trees.

The colorfully painted "barn" that sits in the middle of a circular clearing is decent-sized and adorable. It's clear there are multiple rooms inside. I approach to peek through one of the many windows but find I'd have to hop to see inside.

Damn my short legs.

The main sliding door is cracked open.

"Hello?" I knock firmly and call into the empty room.

There's no answer. At first, I decide that's that and turn to head back down the path I arrived on. But a tingle of curiosity and excitement stops me in my tracks.

What's the harm in taking a quick look around? I won't steal anything, and I know how to keep my hands to myself. A gander won't hurt.

I press open the door expecting it to creak and squeal across the iron rail, but it slides silently. A cursory glance around the clearing shows that I'm still alone so, I quickly slip inside. Once the door shifts back, I finally get a chance to look around the large room.

And I'm instantly affected.

Between the warmth, the sun filtering in through the high windows, and the smell of paint and wood and clay, I'm transported to my early twenties when art filled my life. My mind. The space is peaceful. Dust motes dance around in the beams of light, whirring wildly in the air when they encounter the gently circulating ceiling fans. Colorful splotches adorn most surfaces, including the counters that rim the room. Countless mason jars litter shelves housing paintbrushes of literally every shape and size. I step closer and wrap my fingers around the biggest fan brush I've ever seen.

The bristles are nearly the size of my hand. The canvas someone would put this to would be ginormous. I replace it and continue my exploration with my heart full to the brim with excitement and anticipation.

Buy this point I'm sold. I'm so in for whatever's about to happen here that I'd accept making handprint ornaments or paper mâché piñatas with balloons and newspaper strips.

I'm so ridiculously optimistic that this next week will completely rewire my focus and reignite old passions that seemed long gone. Bring back parts of me I assumed had dried and crumbled away. Reignite whatever has been missing for a very long time. I can feel it somewhere deep in my core.

I let out a little shriek of glee, twirl like a child, and bend forward, flopping my chest to the long butcher block table in the middle of the room. My arms spread wide so that I'm practically hugging the massive oak surface. My content sigh blows minute crayon shavings and tiny bits of thread into the air. Normally, I'd care about the remnants being all over my shirt and in my hair, but at the moment I don't give a single damn.

"Can I help you with something?"

The deep voice is so close and abrupt that shock knocks the wind right out of me. In one fell swoop I rocket to a stand and fling around to be on guard or attack or run. My instincts haven't figured out if it's a fight situation or flight situation quite yet.

And they don't have a chance to recover either, because

in my herky jerky movements, I slam into the source of the voice, eliciting a sharp curse from him.

I feel the water and smell the paint before I see either and already know it's a disaster.

But what I don't expect is a color-splotched shirtless hunk to be standing there with paint brushes, palette, and a shocked expression.

Everett

Astrid had said when she hired me that I could make use of any supplies Evergreen Adventure Camp had on site. Paint, canvas, brushes, clay. If it's there, it's fair game.

But I have expensive tastes.

Not generally, mind you. When you're a relatively under-educated under-skilled twenty-one-year-old guardian to your kid sisters, you learn quickly how to stretch your hard-earned money. I've spent the last eleven years pinching my pennies to make sure Edith and Grace had everything they needed with an occasional want thrown in. There was a lot of corner cutting, especially when it came to any luxuries just for me.

Fortunately, both of my smarty-pants siblings got full-ride scholarships to their colleges and hold down jobs for spending money, which means for once I have a modest budget to use on anything I want.

So, in an irresponsible act of frivolity, I spent every spare cent on canvases, brushes, and the best oil paints I could afford. They aren't top-tier, but the mid-level quality is more than enough for the amount I was willing to splurge.

But as I stare at one of my big ass blank canvases, I wonder if it was an utter waste of money.

I've been standing here for two fucking hours—shirtless, barefoot, in my old painting jeans that are a little snug if I'm being honest, death metal blasting through my headphones —with nothing to show for it. Ok, fine. That's not entirely true. I also have a headache.

My stomach growls and I check my watch. There's enough time for a quick shower before dinner so I might as well call it quits.

I gather the paintbrushes that I'd swirled in paint at some point but never put to the pristine white canvas and tip them into a large mason jar of water.

I'm putting too much pressure on myself.

I haven't painted in over a decade. That's the reason I'm blocked. I can't expect to come off a hiatus that substantial and instantly create a career-making masterpiece. Time and understanding. That's what I need.

That and perhaps a little inspiration.

Full palette in one hand and a jar of paint water in the other, I stride out to the main room to clean up.

And screech to a halt when I see her bent over *my* art table. The most perfect heart-shaped ass perched up on tiptoes. Her adorable little hands reach to either side and pat the scuffed wood like she's giving it a reassuring hug.

Part of me wonders if I should be irked, put out in some way because one of the campers has invaded my space when they weren't invited. But I can't. The position she's in is. . .perfect? Is it weird to think that? I can't see her face, but her body language puts off something I feel in my gut. She's holding some large emotion that I can't quite identify, even though I relate to whatever it is. Because it looks a lot like how I felt walking into this building for the first time.

Like finding home.

I shake my head to banish the silly notion, since I couldn't possibly know what is going through this lady's head. For all I know she's had a few too many drinks already and needed a place to shake off her buzz.

She hasn't noticed me yet. My bare feet don't make much noise as I move closer. I'm an arm's length away and realize I'd better say something because my proximity to her is starting to border on creepy.

"Can I help you with something?" I ask, a smile pulling ferociously at my lips.

I'm not sure who startled whom more.

But the little blonde rockets to a stand and rams into me as she spins. I hiss as the cold paint palette squelches against my chest and water sloshes over the rim of the mason jar.

She stands frozen with a positively horrified expression, hands on either side of her gaped mouth like she was the original inspiration for Edvard Munch's *The Scream*. Her eyes are fixed on my core. They travel no higher than the resulting tapestry of our collision.

There's silence aside from the paintbrushes clattering to the ground and my heart thundering in my ears.

"I'm so sorry. Holy crap, I'm sorry." The words burst

from her with hearty embarrassment. Her neck and cheeks flame scarlet as she looks around, clocking the disaster we've created. The splash must have hit her as well, because muddled water drips from the ends of her hair onto her shirt.

"It's all right," I try to assure, peeling the wooden oval from my skin and marveling at the design left behind. Drips of cloudy water trail from my shoulder down through the smear of contrasting colors, blurring them together like conflicting emotions that somehow make sense. I smirk at the insane impulse to smear myself all over the nearly blank canvas in the back, like the body print would somehow translate the ridiculousness of this situation.

Then the smirk morphs into a laugh.

Her blush deepens and travels further down her chest. My gaze follows the bloom. Even more so as she suddenly peels her top off and steps forward. Before I can stop her, she's wiping her shirt all over my chest, trying desperately to clean up the mess.

"I didn't think anyone was in here," she rambles, voice wobbly and full of texture. Her blonde hair flares gold in the streams of sunlight sneaking in above us. "I had a few minutes before opening ceremonies and wanted to check out the studio before the first session tomorrow. It's been a long, *long* time since I've been around anything creative and the proximity to all these supplies just took over. Before I knew it I had an urge to hug this big table like it was an old friend. Have you ever felt that way?"

"Like hugging a table?" I tease, reaching to the side to toss the smeared palette and mason jar onto the counter nearby. My skin tingles where she touches me. To distract myself, I remove my glasses, which were squarely in the splash zone.

She huffs, actually has the gall to direct a bit of pinched irritation at me, and snatches my filthy glasses. She's trying to wipe them clean, but the paint she collected from my chest makes the lenses even more of a disaster. "No. I mean, feeling overcome with something ineffable?"

Catching her bent over my table comes to mind.

All manner of intrusive thoughts battle for my attention. Like what if we knew each other and she'd surprised me in that very position? Or how she might gasp if I pulled her against my painted chest, dirtying the sheer blue bra she wears. Or something as simple as pressing my fingers beneath her chin so she'll finally look me in the eyes.

I take my smeared eyewear back and swallow, noticing how she watches my throat bob. She moves to resume wiping me down and then seems to melt beneath my touch as I settle a hand on either shoulder and take a step back. My skin instantly mourns the loss of contact.

"Yes, I can most definitely say I've experienced that," I mutter.

"I called out, but no one answered," she says hurriedly, wringing her t-shirt in her fists. Paint tints her fingers with each twist, burying pigment beneath her nails. It will take some effort for her to clean them, and I'm suddenly giddy that she may carry the evidence of our encounter through the rest of her day.

"I was in the back, wearing these." I tap the headphones that hang around my neck.

She finally looks up and I'm unable to hear anything over the way my heart hammers away at my sternum.

This woman is breathtaking. Much more than the parts of her I've already noticed. She's short; the top of her head barely reaches my chin. Her curves beg my fingers to trace them, especially where the thin blue lace cups her full breasts. Her body is everything feminine and lithe, but her face?

Fuck.

This blonde goddess has the features of an angel. Silky skin with cherry cheeks and a dimple that sinks into her chin as she worries her white teeth across her bottom lip. Hints of laugh lines crease the outer edges of her eyes, pointing to a life of humor and happiness. I could swim in her eyes, they're so crystal blue, aside from a tiny gray speck on her left iris. I suddenly feel the urge to devote my entire set of canvases to capturing the colors in her gaze.

How long have I been staring at her? No doubt an awkward amount of time.

She tears her gaze from mine and catalogues the smears of paint on my torso. Each color blends together in a monotonous grayish green coating.

"I made it worse," she chuckles.

I'm helpless to join in the mirth. The situation is just so ridiculous.

"And it appears you've ruined a perfectly good shirt," I respond, pointing to the sloppy fabric bunched in her hands.

She looks down and laughs even harder. "Luckily, I have more."

When our giggles subside, she releases a contented sigh and swipes at a tear that's tipped over her lower lid.

I'm about to ask her name and offer mine. Open my mouth to do so but she lets out an embarrassed squeak first.

"Oh my god," she blurts, eyes going wide as she realizes she's standing there practically topless. Her arms spread across her chest in an effort to restore her modesty.

"I barely saw anything," I assure. Which is a big fat lie. There's no way I couldn't have noticed how see-through this woman's bra is. If they haven't already, poets should write sonnets about the perfect shape of her heavy breasts. About the way her nipples press through the thin lace so invitingly. My mouth waters because I'm suddenly envisioning hoisting her onto the very table she was bent over to feast on her sweetness.

She becomes twitchy—even moreso than a moment ago when she realized she'd ripped off her shirt in order to wipe down a complete stranger. My body turns of its own accord, tracking her as she shuffles toward the sliding door.

"I'd better go clean up," she announces. She pulls the door open, pops her head outside, then wrenches it shut again.

"Here," I snag the white shirt I had tucked in my back pocket and step toward her.

She squeaks again and steps back only to bump into the sliding door.

"No, no. It's fine." She holds out a hand and I stop.

"Really, I'm not using it," I insist.

"Mine's alright." She flips out the fabric to investigate the damage. There's a cringe, followed by a shrug, and finally she resigns to pulling the filthy shirt over her head. It clings to her form and I drink in her seductive curves.

"Better than alright," I say breathlessly, completely lacking the control to keep my thoughts inside my head.

She levels a scowl at me, one meant to chastise, but it only makes me smile wider. The liquid pools of her irises boil over with frustration and I'm instinctually obsessed with assisting her.

"Just in case," I offer while tossing her my shirt. But before she can protest again I turn from her and head to the counter to clean my palette and jar.

There's another little huff, a rustle of cloth, followed by the smooth whisper of the barn door sliding open. "Thanks and sorry again."

I peek over my shoulder. She slips from the Art Barn but not before I catch sight of my shirt draped over her body. The bottom hem nearly reaches her knees and I know I'm a goner.

Stay tuned for the rest of Melody and Everett's story. You won't want to miss Hearts and Crafts, the next book in the Camp Clandestine Series.

Thank you for visiting Camp Clandestine!

If you've enjoyed your stay I welcome you to leave me a review wherever you love talking about books. Each and every star rating, post, and share makes an incredible difference for indie authors like me.

After leaving a review, join my newsletter by heading to my website: www.klparsonsbooks.com to find out what's next at Camp Clandestine and beyond...

Acknowledgments

It seems like only yesterday....

Wait. That's not exactly how I want to start this—even if it DOES seem like only yesterday when I published my first novel, Love by a Landslide. The point I'm trying to make is that the last (almost) two years have been bonkers! Bananas! Truly life changing in all the best ways possible. And I have so many people to thank for it.

I'd be remiss if I didn't start with my incredibly supportive hubby, Dave. You put up with so much that if I could give you a medal I would. Between playing interference with our little dude so I can crank out an extra few words, heading up (ok, fine...completely running) my IT department, and being a good sport about having to buy a copy before I let you read it, you are truly the cinnamon roll hero in my real life grumpy/sunshine romance.

Next, to my fabulous beta readers and IRL besties, Jacki and Tricia, thank you for being the first sets of eyes on my WIPs (that's work in progress for all of you non-writers). I know you'll tell me like it is when something doesn't feel quite right and push me to get my butt in the chair when you're antsy for my next project. Don't worry Jacki, my shifter romance is coming...eventually. I really don't think my finished products would be quite as solid without your feedback and support.

Of course I have to shout out to my lovely, diligent, and flexible editor, Michelle Kowalski. Thank you for whipping my words into shape and cleaning them up for public consumption. No doubt I'd have many readers dip out in the first chapter if it weren't for your sharp eye and talent. Grammar and spelling are hard y'all. And don't get me started on my excessive use of commas and ellipses...

New to my orbit is the wildly talented Sam of Ink and Laurel. I literally welled up with tears when I saw the first color proof of Capture My Flag and I still can't stop staring! Thank you so much for bringing Leilani and Hudson to life on this stunning cover. I'm so freaking excited to see what you do with the next two books.

A big thanks to my sensitivity reader, Michelle Swinea of Inherently Valuable. Your careful analysis of my manuscript is exactly what I needed in order to portray Leilani in a respectful and conscientious way. Thank you for your guidance.

Where's my street team at??? Don't think I forgot about you wonderful humans, because I didn't. Your incredible support makes a huge difference in my publishing efforts. Between the kind words, praise, and assistance in sharing my work with your followers I've been blown away by each of you! Aunt Shirley, Danielle, Shabella, Ana, Emily, Cassie, Katheryn, Fiona, Suzette, Kayli, Jenna, Heidi, Amber, Jules, Robin, and Amanda you all totally rock!

To all the indie authors I've met along the way, or

connect with via chat groups, or in person author group...I see you and appreciate all the tips, tricks, and advice you've shared. It's been an honor hustling beside you the last couple of years. Here's to decades more!

I really hope you all loved Capture My Flag. This story was a blast to write and I can't wait for you to follow along with Melody in the next one. Stay tuned...

About the Author

K. L. Parsons writes about her obsessions, which is why her romances are steeped in humor, adventure, and PNW vibes. When she isn't crafting swoony stories she can be found hiking, climbing, cross stitching snarky patterns, playing the nerdiest of boardgames, reading (90% romance with a few thrillers thrown in), and scurrying from room to room trying to figure out why the hell she walked in there to begin with. She lives in Washington State among the lush evergreens with her husband, son, and doodle named Frank.

Find her on the following socials under the username:

@klparsonsbooks